APOLLO
RHODES

A MAN FOR ALL TIME

DR. PETER PARRAS

First published by Peter Parras Pty Ltd in 2018

A catalogue record for this book is available from the National Library of Australia

Edited by Margie Tubbs

Internal layout by OMNE Author Services
www.omneauthorservices.com.au

Cover by Mihail Uvarov

Printed by OMNE Publishing www.omnepublishing.com.au

This book is available in print and ebook formats.

DISCLAIMER

This book is essentially a work of fiction. However it also contains historical and scientific information based on the author's own knowledge and experience. Except in the case of proven scientific fact, any scientific opinions appearing in this book may be the product of the author's imagination and may be fictitious.

Except in the case of historical fact, any resemblance to actual persons, living or dead, is purely coincidental. Some of the names, characters, places and incidents appearing in this work are the sole expression, opinion and product of the author's imagination only. They may be entirely fictitious and may not represent or be based on any real life views of any character or event in any way whatsoever—any such resemblance is strictly coincidental.

Some of the references to and depictions of real life persons, living or deceased, or organisations, government bodies or institutions, appearing in this work are based solely and entirely on the author's imagination. They do not necessarily represent or bear any resemblance to the actual views or opinions of such persons, institutions, organisations or bodies. Any events relating to the said persons, institutions, organisations or bodies (public or private) depicted in this book may also be fictitious.

This book is designed to provide entertainment, information and motivation to our readers. It is sold with the understanding that the author and publisher are not engaged to render any type of psychological, religious, medical, legal or any other kind professional advice.

The eschatological and religious views expressed in this book by the author are his opinions only. They are purely theoretical and are not meant to represent the views of any particular religious organisation or group.

DEDICATION

This book is dedicated to my wonderful wife and soulmate, Maria, without whose unswerving support and infinite patience, it could not have been written. This story is also the product of the inspiration and encouragement I have received, over many years, from our three amazingly devoted and loving children without whom life, for us, would be meaningless.

THE STORY FOR THIS BOOK CAME TO ME IN A DREAM
THAT I EXPERIENCED SEVERAL YEARS AGO. ITS IMPACT
HAS NEVER LEFT ME. I BELIEVE IT WAS INSPIRED BY A
HIGHER POWER THAT IS AVAILABLE TO ALL OF US.

GET READY TO BE ENTERTAINED
AND UPLIFTED AS YOU READ ON.

Peter Parras

CONTENTS

PROLOGUE

Question:

What are the most oft-asked questions of every person who has ever lived or is yet to live?

Answer:

Where am I going when I die? What is to become of me and my loved ones?

It is no accident or coincidence that you have selected this book to read. You have been drawn to this story by a force much greater than you or me; but the force has been activated by your insatiable thirst for wisdom and truth which will last for the rest of your earthly existence. It is only when you have *shuffled off this mortal coil* (to quote Shakespeare) that all will be made clear to you. The story, the events and the treasury of wisdom that this narrative will reveal to you should be known to all. I believe that you, the reader, have an obligation to inform your family, friends and acquaintances of the existence of this book.

Does the world really need another hero? There are already many so-called heroes in the world today—men and women in uniform, people in authority, heads of government, politicians and leaders of all kinds. However, with the ever-burgeoning waves of crime, drug trafficking, rampant drug abuse, human trafficking and sexual exploitation (among other daily transgressions of human rights too numerous to list here), I believe we do need another hero. But we need a new type of hero: one that is unique and different from anyone the world has experienced before. We need one that combines special qualities, talents, abilities and powers with old-world virtues, morality, ethical standards and decency. Yes, emphatically and unequivocally, the world needs such a hero!

This is the story of that hero. Prepare to be exhilarated, enlightened, edified, emotionally moved and, above all, thoroughly satisfied as you read on.

CHAPTER I
A MAN CALLED APOLLO

Dark, foreboding rain clouds gathered in the late afternoon sky to eclipse the low-lying sun, as it struggled to impart its dwindling beams of light and warmth to the city below. The distant crash of thunder reverberated ominously in the firmament. A sudden flash of lightning momentarily lit up the gloomy sky above the home of Apollo Rhodes and his bedridden mother, Maria.

Apollo's mother was quite ill. It was imperative that Apollo get to the drugstore as soon as possible to have the doctor's prescription dispensed.

In the course of her illness, Apollo's mother had been ruminating about the past. There were a few things she wanted to get off her chest. The apprehension aroused by her illness made her believe that **now** was the right time to bring them up. 'You've been a good boy for your mom all these years since your father died. And it hasn't been easy—it's been downright tough. You were only a teenager when your father passed.

'You know, Apollo, I recently came across a few things that I'd actually forgotten about. They're kind of memorabilia from your father's life: keepsakes and mementos. There are also a few things your dad wanted you to have when you got a bit older. I think it's about time you saw them.'

Glancing at the clock, Maria paused and, with a pensive expression and a furrowed brow, reconsidered: 'Maybe we can talk about this later, when I'm feeling better and you have more time. You'd better get off to the drugstore now. And be careful, sweetheart—it may be about to rain. I think I heard thunder too ... I love you son.'

Apollo responded to his mother with a degree of curiosity combined with an element of concern: 'Sure, we can talk later. I love you too ma—very much. Don't worry ma, I'll be fine. It's only a few blocks to the drugstore. I'll be there and back before the rain starts.'

Apollo quickly departed on foot, knowing that if he hurried he might be able to avoid the fury of the storm which seemed imminent. Having purchased his mother's medication, he proceeded to return. Looking outside the drugstore, Apollo observed light rain which did not concern him. Claps of thunder and distant flashes of lightning accompanied him as he made a dash along the street. His long legs carrying his thin, six foot frame were, however, insufficient to protect him against the devastating speed of the lightning bolt that descended upon his body from on high. The event was not observed by any other pedestrians, so quickly did it happen. However, as Apollo fell to the ground stupefied by the effect of the lightning, passers-by came to his aid and found him unconscious.

MY STORY

I was born Apollo Rhodes in Washington DC, 29 years ago. My parents, both of diverse European backgrounds, were also born in the United States. My father died of cancer when I was in my early teens. Unfortunately, we didn't get to know each other as well as we might have, because dad was always busy with work. He tried to make up for it in the last nine months of his life and he left me a lot of wonderful memories and legacies in writing and in photographs which I'll always treasure. There may be some items held by my mother that I have yet to see. She put them away until I was 'old enough' to appreciate them, so she said. There may also be things that have been put in 'a safe place' and then forgotten. Time will tell what comes to light.

My mother still lives in the suburbia of Washington DC. Being an only child, my relationship with my mother is extremely close. She's not only a wonderful mother, but also my best friend and confidante. I often stay with her, especially when she needs me, but I also have a residence closer to my office.

Several years ago I graduated from George Washington University with a Science degree majoring in zoology, medical science and criminology. I have been in the employ of the US government since graduating, but the department I work in is classified.

Everyone has heard of adults and children being struck by lightning—the weather in the US and other parts of the world can be so unpredictable! Details of such calamitous events are often in the daily news reports. There is invariably little time to avoid the devastating effect of lightning strikes.

It's not unusual for the victim of a lightning strike to die on the spot. Others may be more fortunate and receive only a nasty shock, but are otherwise unscathed and physically unchanged. In my case, I survived with very unusual consequences.

After I was struck by lightning, I was rendered comatose for many months and remained on life support in one of Washington DC's major hospitals. Most of the information that I'm about to relate is based on my firsthand knowledge. For other details, I am grateful for the input given to me by my attending neurologist, the eminent Prof. Carl Sandberg, who, along with his specialist team, cared for me throughout those crucial months following my injury. This is my story—one that just had to be told.

I am the principal narrator but, from time to time, Prof. Sandberg will be the storyteller. He is the medical professional in whom I have confided the most. Bound by professional confidentiality, Prof. Sandberg will only reveal information that he and I have agreed is essential to the story, but all will be revealed in the fullness of time.

What occurred during my months of hospitalization, and in the subsequent months that followed my release from hospital, can only be described as defying all present and past human understanding of the brain and the way it functions (for further insights into the human brain see Appendix 1). It also flies in the face of everything that we have come to expect, from our past experiences, about major and direct trauma from lightning strikes on human beings.

Not only did I survive the lightning strike, but it gradually became apparent that I was a changed man. To me, it seems that changes continue to evolve and reveal themselves in different ways to this very day. At first, the changes were subtle and difficult to define or to explain. Only now am I partially beginning to comprehend what has happened to me as a person, as well as who I really am in the great scheme of things.

My perception and understanding of birth, death, life and eternity have slowly but distinctly been revealed to me on a daily basis, as my brain and my thinking have changed as a result of that fateful day. I cannot explain it. Nobody can explain it. I know what is true and I will reveal those facts in the hope that you will read on with an open mind. With such receptivity you will begin to appreciate concepts, ideas and beliefs which may be foreign to you now, but which you may later embrace gladly, as a source of hope and comfort for your present and future life. Your understanding and appreciation of life beyond death— which to many is just seen as an oblivion of darkness and non-existence—will be greatly enhanced.

CHAPTER 2
DREAMS AND VISIONS

Among the first things that I can recall a few weeks after the accident, while still in my profound comatose state, was a sense of deep sleep visited intermittently by dreams, sometimes good and sometimes bad, as in a typical nightmare. From the point of view of the intensive care nursing and medical staff, I appeared to be virtually brain-dead. They could not detect much brainwave activity nor could they elicit any peripheral reflex responses from me, despite substantial physical and verbal stimuli. However, nothing could have been further from the truth. In fact, in the weeks that followed, it appeared that my brain was not only beginning to reactivate, but that it was opening up to a higher level, which I could not possibly have imagined before the accident.

There were times when I seemed to be having out of body experiences. I could see what was happening in my room from the vantage point of my spirit being (see Appendix 2 Principles of Eschatology). I could see exactly what the staff were doing and I could hear what they were saying. Many times negative statements were spoken due to ignorance. Occasionally, positive words of hope were uttered by the doctors in answer to questions from my vigilant mother and concerned relatives and friends who were visiting me.

As it turned out, the medication meant for my mother was found in my possession by the ambulance men and it was kindly delivered to her. She was then informed of my accident, much to her horror. Fortunately, she did recover from her ailment, while keeping vigil over me at the hospital.

As the weeks became months, my neurological charts revealed that my level of responsiveness was beginning to improve. Although still not conscious, I was responding to external physical stimuli and I was beginning to respond to auditory stimulation, i.e., sound.

Several weeks later, reports from the nurses' clinical notes indicated that I was beginning to vocalize and eventually verbalize in my sleep. However, as my verbalizing became clearer and more distinct, one very unusual observation was consistently made by different nursing staff. The perplexing observation was that I was not speaking in English—but it was the only language I'd ever known, as my parents only spoke English to me. Furthermore, I had never studied languages in high school and had never been overseas. In fact, I was speaking in what seemed to be several different languages, some of which not even multilingual observers could identify!

Another interesting phenomenon was becoming apparent in the course of my hospital treatment. Immediately after my accident, MRI scans performed in hospital appeared to indicate major areas of brain damage, including some areas of possible infarction (brain death). Naturally, such an initial adverse finding did not augur well for any level of recovery. The prognosis offered to my mother for a full recovery was naturally poor, based on the MRI findings.

However, as the months passed by and I seemed to be improving, a follow-up MRI miraculously showed that not only were there no areas of infarction, but that the areas of the brain responsible for memory, intuition, language and verbal skills, concentration and learning had actually expanded in size, compared with the rest of the brain. From the MRI, other areas of the brain had in no way diminished and had not been compromised in any way.

At about the six-month mark, I regained my full and normal level of consciousness. However, I was exceptionally weak and my muscles had become atrophied due to inactivity for such a long time. I required physical therapy and rehabilitation.

Prof Sandberg later revealed to me some candid clinical observations that he had recorded at the time, apropos my physical and psychological condition.

PROF. SANDBERG PROFILES APOLLO

Apollo is a young man looking no older than twenty-nine. He is approximately 6 feet tall with a well-proportioned physique, but is lean with poor musculature not helped by the fact that he has been bedridden for six months. He has an abundance of medium to dark brown hair and light-colored eyes, best described as blue-green. He has an engaging smile which displays straight white teeth and adherence to meticulous oral hygiene.

Prof Sandberg also opined (without neces-sarily making a written record) that Apollo could be described by some observers as classically good-looking, given his well-proportioned facial features: a straight nose, unobtrusive ears and strong jaw. He also observed that Apollo appeared to be a good soul with a pleasant, affable and polite manner. As his interaction with the nursing staff increased with improving health, Apollo demonstrated a great respect for women and those in authority, especially the elderly.

At this stage, I was oblivious to my episodes of sleep talking, as amusingly related to me by the staff. Nor could I recall any details of my dream states. On the other hand, my out of body experiences were distinct and clear. However, I was reluctant to discuss them with the hospital staff, as I anticipated that such reports would be met with the usual smirks of disbelief and just dismissed as hallucinatory episodes.

My main thought was that, despite all of the ominous and unfavorable predictions regarding my prognosis, I had been very lucky to survive. I had made a proverbial 'miraculous recovery' from what was often a fatal event. Above all, I was extremely grateful that I had not been left with a permanent disability. I erroneously believed that, after a period of rehabilitation, my life would return to what it was before the accident. To restate two oft-quoted clichés: nothing could have been further from the truth and nothing could have prepared me for what was to follow.

CHAPTER 3
TECHNICOLOR DREAMS

In my final weeks of convalescence in the hospital and during the week that followed my return to home life, I began to encounter extremely vivid dreams on a nightly basis. However, they were dreams of a kind that I had never previously experienced. As each night passed, the dreams became more real and more distinct. The colors in these dreams became brighter and more vivid. The pictures that I saw in my sleeping state became clearer and more precise. It was as if I was living out my dreams, because most of the time I formed a part of them.

Those dreams were not fleeting, illogical and fanciful events that one vaguely remembers after waking. They were more like informative and instructive documentaries (in technicolor) of events, occurrences and incidents at various times from the past and which, in some way, involved me or people known to me. These dreams, although mystifying, in no way bothered me. In fact, I welcomed my sleep and I began to look forward to the next night's presentation, as a child would eagerly await the next instalment of his favorite movie serial.

However, with time, I began to experience an interesting progression of my nocturnal dreams—in the course of my diurnal activities, I would suddenly see, in my mind's eye, clear visions like color photography. These visions, again, appeared to be events from bygone days; in some cases, they seemed to be quite familiar; in other cases, they were totally foreign to me. My puzzlement increased as these images continued to manifest over the ensuing weeks.

As the months passed and I attempted to return to my usual everyday life, the dreams and visions became exhaustingly frequent and seemed to take over my whole life to the point of distraction. I was seeing people and events, seemingly from past eras, with whom and with which I felt some sort of connection and familiarity. But at the same time, I could not explain the reason for those feelings. Naturally, I surmised that I could have no possible association with them, due to my relatively young age. It was as though I was watching a movie that I must have seen before, but I had no recollection of when or where I had seen it.

BACK TO HOSPITAL

I decided to consult my neurologist in an attempt to get an explanation for what I was experiencing. Even with his vast experience, Prof. Sandberg was also perplexed, but he suggested that I return to the hospital to be observed overnight as I slept. Under such observation, it appeared that I was again talking in my sleep. However, this time, according to the observers, my enunciation appeared to be clearer. There was no doubt that I was, in fact, speaking in different languages during the course of the night. But, as mentioned before, I was in no way multilingual and could only speak English.

Naturally, as I was asleep at the time, I was not aware of what I had said, nor of the languages I had spoken. Nevertheless, after the various languages were revealed to me, there appeared to be some correlation with the events in my dream. Two of the languages could not be identified with certainty. The others appeared to be Italian, German, French and, of course, English. I was beginning to become apprehensive, as I felt that I might be losing my mind.

Prof. Sandberg decided to perform another MRI of my brain to see whether he could detect any changes compared to those previously observed in hospital. He was surprised to find that two parts of the brain which play a crucial role in memory, namely the hippocampus and the amygdala, had grown even larger than previously. As Prof. Sandberg described it, it was as though the brain was making more room for its memory retrieving elements at the expense of other areas of the brain which were already in plentiful supply and could afford some shrinkage. Yet the burning question remained: what was causing this phenomenon to take place? If anything, the changes were clearly improvements on an already normal brain which had been affected by a lightning strike. Prof. Sandberg could not see any abnormal pathology and therefore merely advised me to go home and continue my normal life. He suggested that I return periodically to see him in his office.

CHAPTER 4
THE NEW APOLLO

I couldn't complain as I was not ill, but I couldn't help wondering where all of this was heading. I returned to my usual federal government job in the city and I was going through the motions of my work. Up to this point in my life I had never been particularly athletic, nor had I engaged in physical exercise or sporting activities with any sense of passion or zeal. However, some weeks after leaving hospital for the sleep study, I started to experience emotions, feelings, desires and inclinations that I had not previously felt. Inexplicably, I felt a strong urge to work out in the local gym. I even started to show an interest in sports generally, but particularly in body contact sports such as wrestling, boxing and football.

I had been conscientious in my studies at high school, but I had never been successful in sport. I was the sort of guy that you would probably pick last in your team or keep on the bench as a reserve. I just didn't seem to have the robust physical attributes and coordination necessary to excel in a particular sport. As a result, I just gave up trying. Some people might have called me a klutz for want of a better description.

I had always been what one might call a timid or shy person, perhaps even introverted. A good word to describe me would be 'diffident', because I also lacked self-confidence. I'd never been the one who would speak up in a crowd or volunteer for activities outside my comfort zone. I was a quiet and peaceful person, who would rather avoid confrontation than risk life or limb—my own or other people's. I believed that I was a good, decent and caring person, but I wouldn't risk getting involved in life-threatening situations. I would seldom venture out at night alone.

I had never held a gun, used a knife or weapon of any kind. I had never taken classes in self-defense and I had no knowledge of boxing, judo, karate or any other martial art. Indeed, I had no inclination to do so.

It seemed in a way that I was changing as a person. I felt as though I was being torn between my old inner self: the peaceful and caring, yet uninvolved, young man, content to go through the motions of life by playing it safe and being satisfied with an average mediocre existence; while, on the other hand, I was starting to feel an inner call, deep in my soul. This irresistible call beckoned me to go further, to do more and to explore beyond my comfort zone, even if it meant that danger and risk were lurking around every corner.

People who knew me noticed a change in me. Although some might have thought that I was gravitating towards the so-called 'dark side', I knew that this was not so. I knew that the inherent good nature with which I was born, and the love of my fellow man that had been nurtured by my parents, still remained strong in my spirit and would endure beyond anything that tried to change it.

In general terms, I was certainly becoming a more physical person, which had never previously been my inclination. I was now more inclined to walk rather than drive and to engage in physical exercises that would previously have been unpalatable to me. But beyond that, I was also becoming more competitive and more aggressive in a healthy, non-belligerent way.

ON THE ROAD TO A NEW AND IMPROVED BODY AND MIND

I started to attend a gym close to my work. I had never previously been a zealot of fitness but, for the first time in my life, I was really keen to train and I enjoyed it. My physical reflexes became quicker than I had previously experienced. It was a personality change, and I began to realize that the lightning strike had brought about many changes in my life. At this point, I could only go along with what my brain was telling me to do.

My physical body and my desire to improve it were changing for the better, but it also appeared that my mind was becoming sharper. My attention to detail was keener than before and my memory seemed to be more retentive. I was able to recall things from my childhood that previously had faded from my memory altogether. It was as though I was remembering them for the first time, but I knew, without a shadow of a doubt, that they had occurred, no matter how trivial those events were.

I also seemed to be curious and inquisitive about anything in particular and all things in general. If something that I had not heard about before was covered on the evening news, I was intent on learning about it. So keen was my desire to learn and to understand, people accused me of being obsessional. I was also fastidious about time and punctuality.

The French phrase *déjà vu* refers to that feeling you get when you're doing or seeing something that you have experienced before. However, the feeling is so vague that you tend to dismiss it as just your imagination. I was experiencing feelings of *déjà vu* almost every day. I continued to experience visual images in my brain, some of which were still photographs and others moving pictures.

CHAPTER 5
ON DANGEROUS GROUND

In the course of my employment, I would sometimes be required to travel around the greater Washington DC area. Prior to my accident, my instinct had been to avoid venturing into neighborhoods that were unfamiliar to me. Because my personality had previously gravitated towards self-preservation, I had been able to manipulate my duties to avoid the possibility of physical confrontation and personal danger. However, I now found myself taking on a new persona in which adventure and risk-taking were unbridled. I had become more cavalier about the possibility of danger lurking in unknown territory. It was an attitude which had been foreign to me prior to the lightning strike, but now everything seemed to be changing.

For no rational reason, I became more confident in stepping out and boldly dealing with the possibility of danger. It was the sort of attitude exhibited by teenagers who volunteer for war believing they are bulletproof and looking forward to the front line as an opportunity to see the world and savor a taste of adventure. The possibility of death is seemingly relegated to the back of their minds and somehow suppressed. The irrationality of such thinking is clearly understood by concerned parents and more mature family members as they reluctantly farewell the all-too-eager teenage army volunteers.

In my moments of reflection and contemplation as a relatively mature man in his late 20s, I knew that I was not impervious to harm. Nevertheless, just like the dare-devil motorcycle rider who is prepared to leap over several buses in flames to demonstrate his prowess and bask in the adulation of an excited crowd of onlookers, I too seemed prepared to accept the possibility of danger in order to enjoy the thrill of adventure. This feeling was new to me and, although I was puzzled as to why I was thinking like this, my overwhelming gut instinct was to embrace rather than reject it.

It was with this newly acquired state of mind that I found myself venturing into an area of Washington DC that was totally foreign to me and one which the old Apollo Rhodes would never have visited.

Everyone is familiar with the tendency for gangs to evolve in the large communities of major cities throughout the United States and the world generally, especially where there are multiple ethnic or racial groups. These gangs can be violent in their defense of what they regard as their designated territory. They are usually not open to the idea of rational discussion if an unsuspecting interloper trespasses into their domain. One might call it the law of the jungle or survival of the fittest. Unfortunately law enforcement agencies cannot be present at all times to protect unsuspecting, naïve individuals who place themselves in harm's way.

In my eagerness to carry out my job and with my newfound devil-may-care disposition, I unsuspectingly wandered into an area of the city where gangs were rife. I had also lost track of time and, as the sun was setting, the shadows of the tall buildings were lengthening, creating dark street corners which the city lights could not completely illuminate.

With a sense of urgency, I quickened my steps in order to find the nearest taxicab. Suddenly I was confronted by four ominous-looking youths, intent on blocking my path. There were no passers-by on whom I might have relied for assistance or support. As I could not get around them, I decided that discretion was the better part of valor and began to retreat to a safer area. Unfortunately, as I did so, my way of escape was again blocked by three more unsavory teenagers, who also seemed intent on doing me harm—I was trapped!

I was surrounded by seven youths who I reasoned were intent on robbing me of my possessions or, worse still, my life. Prior to my lightning encounter which produced my inexplicable character transformation and my new attitude towards physical combat, I undoubtedly would have been paralyzed with fear and rendered a quivering mass of cowardly flesh. Now, although afraid and in a degree of panic, I knew that I could not allow trepidation to immobilize me.

Apart from minor skirmishes in the playground as a child, I had never really been in a position where I needed to defend myself for fear of being harmed. Hitherto, I had led a sheltered life free of violence. But now the walls of protection were down. I was in danger of suffering serious physical harm, perhaps death, at the hands of these thugs.

I was dressed in a conservative suit and tie, carrying a briefcase. Accordingly, I was at odds with their underprivileged socio-economic subculture. I was being targeted as easy prey on whom they could vent their suppressed anger and frustration. At the same time, the thugs might have thought that some of the accessories of modern life, of which they felt unfairly deprived, could now be misappropriated for themselves.

As I looked into their ominous faces, I decided that I was not going to lie down and die, but that I would fight back. With my newly found passion for martial arts, I threw myself into my defense with an exuberance and a vigor that I had never felt before. I swung my briefcase around, using it as a weapon of offence and defense. I took one of them by surprise with the force of the blow and knocked him off his feet. I tripped another one with a sharp kick to his leg. At that point, I thought there was an opening through which I could make a dash to safety. But alas, I was overwhelmed by the sheer number of assailants who quickly descended upon me.

After several punches to my head from different angles, a feeling of faintness descended over me and I fell to the ground. The back of my head struck the pavement with a force that could have fractured my skull. I was unconscious as my spirit-being rose over my body, hovering above me, witnessing all that subsequently transpired.

As the young hoodlums stood over my motionless body in the elation of their victory, an evil looking middle-aged man, who had been lurking all the while in the background, stepped out of the shadows and slowly walked towards me. The young men seemed to acknowledge his presence with a deference that appeared to be generated by fear and obeisance, rather than true respect.

My spirit-man observed that he was a rotund, stocky man with a receding hair line. He had an unhealthy, ruddy complexion, as is often caused by excessive alcohol consumption. He gestured to the leader of the group of assailants to give him my briefcase and wallet. In my briefcase he found a copy of the daily newspaper and only one official document which was non-specific but indicated that I was probably a government employee.

He went through my wallet finding a small amount of cash which he tossed among the group of cutthroats, along with my watch, for them to fight over. He kept my driver's license and a recently expired credit card, no doubt in order to check my identity. He then instructed the leader of the group to dispose of the empty wallet and brief case.

He peered down on my motionless body with a sardonic smirk of indifference and disdain. He then produced a gun from a holster under his coat, with the seeming intent of putting a bullet in my head. At that point, sirens from several police vehicles were heard echoing throughout the immediate vicinity. Fortunately, as a result of the noise of the scuffle, a Good Samaritan in a tenanted building close to the scene had called the police. With the sirens blaring and getting closer by the second, the callous man paused momentarily, reconsidered his intent and returned his gun to its holster.

With speed surprising for his ponderous body habitus, the man disappeared into the recesses of the surrounding buildings with his teenage followers close behind. Only a few minutes later, the police were hovering over me looking for signs of life. An ambulance arrived and transported me to the nearest emergency hospital. I was alive, but remained unconscious.

Chapter 6
My Amazing Spirit-Man

With my physical body motionless in the ambulance, my spirit-man rose to a height that I had never previously experienced, even in hospital after my lightning accident. I wondered (in my spirit-being) whether the adrenalin surge, fueled by the life-threatening, combative nature of the attack on my physical being, may have been a factor.

The term 'astral travel' is often used to describe the feeling of your spirit-being leaving the body and soaring into the cosmos. This term describes the sense that I felt as my spirit soared into another realm, dominated by a white light of magnificent effulgence. I felt calm and at peace with an all-embracing sense of unconditional love drawing me ever closer to the source of the light. But suddenly an avuncular figure, with piercing bright eyes and a gentle but unambiguous hand gesture, directed me to go back and to no longer seek the light—for one brief moment I thought it was the face of my father! With a sense of regret, but also with unwavering obedience, my spirit altered its course with the objective of returning to my physical being.

As I returned to my body, a darkness momentarily descended upon the spirit consciousness that I had just experienced. I awoke with a jolt. I was lying on a makeshift bed of lambskin and covered by a woven blanket of wool. My sickbed seemed to be located in a tent.

As I lay in the tent trying to regain my sense of time (it was like waking from a deep sleep and being temporarily unable to determine the day or time), I could hear the sound of shouting, punctuated by occasional high-pitched screaming in the distance, as well as the faint clanging and crashing of metal upon metal.

It was suddenly revealed to me in my unconscious physical state, without a scintilla of doubt, that my spirit-man had lived before in another body at another time. I was born Paris Apollo in 509 BC in Sparta, Greece.

RECOLLECTION OF THE SPIRIT

What is described here is 'a recollection of the spirit', ie. a true and accurate account of what my spirit had experienced in a past life. This ability of my spirit to remember a past existence in exact detail arose due to a freakish change in my DNA caused by the lightning shock. I've not heard of this ever happening to anyone else.

As I lay there, memories of my Spartan childhood came flooding back to me. I recounted in my mind the love of my mother, the sternness of my father and the grueling training and dedication to duty as a soldier that had finally brought me to this day. It was the year 480 BC. My life flashed before my eyes as an ominous feeling of impending doom overwhelmed me.

My Spartan wife

I then remembered the woman who I had married only a year before—my beloved Amara. She was the love of my life. Her silken, golden chestnut hair and green-blue eyes had captivated me from the very first time I had beheld her when she was but a teenager. I knew then that one day she would be my wife.

By arrangement with our families, we had been betrothed. She was young and nubile. As she smiled welcomingly at me, the dazzling gleam of her brilliant white teeth was only surpassed by the shimmering glow of her almond-shaped, opal-colored orbs. When her eyes met mine in a momentary fixed gaze, it was as though the lightning bolts of Zeus coursed down my whole body to the very tips of my toes.

Her full rosy-red lips, combined with her inviting tongue, delivered the soft feminine voice of a goddess. Her kiss would have made the gods envious, if they had known her as intimately as I. Her voluptuous breasts, curvaceous buttocks and long slim legs delighted me every morning, as she rose from our bed. I recalled wistfully how the sunlight filtering through our window would dance over her swaying, gorgeous locks of hair.

But Amara possessed more than just physical beauty— she had a caring and selfless nature, uncommon in women gifted with such extraordinary pulchritude. She was never conceited, vain or self-consumed.

It was with mixed emotions that I had recently said farewell to my beloved wife. I was overjoyed at the news that she would give birth to our child in eight months but deeply saddened by the possibility that I would never see my unborn child.

As part of the Spartan contingent of some three hundred men under the command of King Leonidas, I was going off to meet the invading army of Xerxes of Persia at the pass of Thermopylae. We all knew in the depths of our souls that we were embarking on a virtual suicide mission. We were facing the largest force of armed men that the world had ever seen. By the same token, as Spartans, we were the most formidable warriors that the world had ever known. But against such a vast enemy with unlimited resources, the odds of victory were definitely against us.

From childhood, I and my Spartan comrades had been taught to have no fear of anything, especially an enemy. We eschewed the easy life and luxury. We embraced deprivation and hardship. We were trained to have no fear of pain or death. As elite Spartan hoplites (foot soldiers) we had been inculcated with the mindset of expectation of victory, because of our superior full-time warrior training.

Despite all my training, I found it hard to hide my feelings as I kissed my wife goodbye, knowing that I would probably not return. We were professional soldiers and our wives were expected to be the bearers of boys who would become future warriors. They knew that their husbands could return from battle in only one of two ways: either carrying their shields or lying on their shields, dead or wounded.

My wife and I loved each other with a passion not often seen in our culture. This made parting all the more difficult. My professional training demanded that I go to war with a zeal that would put fear into the enemy, but deep in my soul I longed to stay with Amara. And her feelings were similar to mine.

As I departed with my Spartan comrades, Amara embraced me with a tearful kiss that almost broke my warrior's heart. It was like a javelin piercing my chest. I will never forget her look of anguish and despair which she attempted to conceal with a poignant half-smile of forlorn hope. At that moment, I loved Amara more than I had ever loved her before.

She knew in her heart of hearts that she might never see me alive again. I suspected the same, but my training was unchallengeable—neither retreat nor defeat were in my vocabulary. I could not show any sign of fear or hesitation.

I had been taught that if death in battle came my way, my reward would be the Elysian Fields, where I would live in eternal bliss with my fellow warriors. But would I eventually be reunited with my beloved Amara there? Would I ever see or know my unborn child? These questions tortured my soul as I ventured forth with my comrades to fight the battle of our lives, in the desperate defense of our homeland against an evil empire.

Before our small force of valiant warriors marched off into glory, we all paid homage to our gods through prayer and supplication. We particularly sought the divine protection and guidance of Apollo and Ares.

We were vastly outnumbered by the enemy, beyond our ability to count. We relied on the tactical advantage of the narrow pass of Thermopylae to minimize the enemy's numerical advantage. As superior warriors, this strategy served us well for a time. We inflicted huge losses upon Xerxes' forces, while suffering only minimal casualties ourselves. However, we were betrayed by one of our own—a traitor who favored self-en-richment with ill-gotten gold over the love of his homeland and his people. That despicable renegade revealed an old goat track to the enemy, by which they could circumvent the pass and then attack us from the rear.

The tent in which I had found myself was designated for those who were severely wounded or those who had fought continuously for an extreme length of time and required rest to regain their strength. I fell into the latter group. Having rested adequately, it was now time for me to return to the fray. However, surrounded by an ever-increasing number of enemy soldiers, our dwindling numbers were doomed, and the battle was lost. No amount of courage, fighting skill or military tactics could avail.

In one last heroic, but vain defense, in the final minutes of the battle, we locked our shields together to fend off the sky-blackening rain of arrows. But our shields were too few and the arrows too many. As the hail of arrows eventually found their mark, our shields fell to the ground, one by one, leaving defenseless the few of us who remained.

Xerxes then sent in his elite troops, the so-called 'Immortals', to deliver the *coup de grâce*. Only a handful of us remained alongside our sovereign, King Leonidas, but we fought bravely and gallantly with what little strength remained in our bodies.

After dispatching several of the Immortals in hand-to-hand combat during one last flurry of defiance, I felt the sting of several arrows as they pierced the flesh of my chest. Falling to my knees, gasping for breath, a generalized weakness overwhelmed my body causing me to drop my sword.

Finally, I felt the impact of a javelin in my back entering through my rib cage. With my last few breaths I cried out, though knowing she could not hear me: 'My darling Amara, I love you. I will always love you. I will love you forever—even in death!'

As I exhaled my last breath, I gave up the ghost. At that very moment my wife awoke suddenly from a deep sleep in a state of panic. She ran to her mother with whom she was staying in my absence, crying frantically: 'He's gone, he's gone! Apollo is dead. I can sense it. The battle is lost.'

'The gods must be telling you this, my dear,' replied her mother. 'It is not possible to know such a thing when the battle is so far away.'

As my spirit ascended, leaving my wounded and lifeless physical body behind, I experienced a freedom that I had never known before. In the blink of an eye, I was transported from the battlefield to my beloved wife, who I found weeping uncontrollably in the comfort of her mother's arms. I knew I could not communicate with her directly, but I was consumed with the knowledge that she would be alright in her earthly life, until we were reunited in the spiritual realm. By some means, I also knew that she would give birth to a son who would grow up to be a great and courageous warrior, as his father had been.

So strong was Amara's love for me and my love for her that I became aware that she could sense my spiritual presence. I knew that she would grieve for a season and that her grief would be profound. Such is the price one pays for loving so deeply in the physical life.

I conjured up a breath of wind and, with the help of Aphrodite, some immaculate white doves to communicate with my beloved from the spirit realm. However, I could not be sad, as I was overwhelmed by the sheer love and joy that was drawing me to heavenly places.

Before I reached the dazzling white light of my eternal home, I woke up in a lather of perspiration, verbalizing in Ancient Greek, much to the astonishment of the hospital staff.

THE SEVEN PROPHECIES
(imparted to Paris Apollo by the Oracle of Delphi)

When Paris Apollo was a boy, his mother took him to the Pythian Oracle several times to learn about his future. The seven pronouncements were as follows:

1. **Neither Gaea's children, nor Poseidon's brood, nor heirs born of the Twins of Leto shall ever harm the chosen one who is worthy of the gods' protection.**

2. **Love will be lost and love regained; love never dies, but ever remains—in the heart of the one who is faithful and true. Look to Eros (beware his arrows, lest your love be misdirected) and Aphrodite for the love that is yours. And this shall be the sign of it: the doves and sparrows.**

3. **The dream that you seek will never die and will be achieved as long as you keep your eye on the prize. Never stop believing in your visions and dreams. Morpheus will visit you to shape your dreams. Never give up, though the odds be high and the enemy nigh. Your belief in yourself and your perseverance will be rewarded by the gods, in the fullness of time.**

4. **The thunderbolt of Zeus, though deadly to mortal man, will in no way harm the hero designated by the gods. Asclepius will make you stronger than before.**

5. **A standard will be raised in a desolate place, though not by you. But in the fullness of time, you shall raise it in the land that you love.**

6. **In the midst of men's evil deeds, you will be the light that pierces the darkness in the name of Apollo and Elpis. A wondrous spear of great mystery will wound the innocent lamb but will bring down a tyrant by your hand alone.**

7. **The winged enforcers of Zeus, the children of Pallas and Styx, shall also be your allies in desperate times; while Heracles, the god of heroes, will strengthen your arm with his mighty power in your hour of need.**

As you read on, see if you can identify the fulfillment of each prophecy.

For further insights into Greek mythology and the Spartans, readers are invited to read Appendix 3.

Chapter 7
DNA—The Key

had been transported to the hospital where records confirmed that I'd previously been under the care of Prof. Sandberg. I remained in that hospital for several days before regaining consciousness.

It appeared that I had been talking in a rambling and delirious manner in my semiconscious state. However, according to the nursing staff and Prof. Sandberg, who also overheard my ramblings, I had not been talking in English, but in a foreign language not familiar to anyone within earshot of my sickbed.

Another MRI had been ordered by Prof. Sandberg and it fortunately revealed no fracture to the skull. The changes previously noted following my lightning accident continued to be evident, if not more pronounced. I had suffered a sufficiently heavy blow to render me unconscious, but fortunately not severe enough to cause a fracture, subarachnoid hemorrhage or a subdural hematoma—maybe I had started to develop a thicker skull!

However, one thing was different. My memory was improving dramatically. In fact, I could remember everything of my life in Sparta all those centuries ago, as though it were yesterday. But I was not ready to reveal this to anyone, including Prof. Sandberg, as I felt I would probably be viewed as some sort of delusional fantasist.

I had learnt from my research into the scientific literature, and from information conveyed to me piecemeal by Prof. Sandberg, that the different types of DNA in our physical make-up determine whether we are susceptible or immune to certain diseases.

We really are in the seminal stage of our understanding of DNA, the types of DNA that we carry and how we all carry different genes for different physical and mental qualities and attributes. We are also now learning that we can turn on and off good or bad genes with DNA switches called regulatory DNA by diet, meditation and exercise.

Clearly, in my case, the lightning strike had serendipitously impacted my regulatory DNA to switch on the genes in my brain which are responsible for memory. This had occurred in a positive and constructive way, by allowing me to recall, in my present earthly existence, events and memories that my spirit-man had experienced in a past physical life.

I would soon learn that the vivid and detailed memories of a past life and my experiences in that life could and would generate definitive changes in my present physical body. These changes would be reflected in remarkable improvement in my musculature, physical prowess and reflexes commensurate with the abilities I had achieved in the past, as evidenced by the memories which were continuing to inundate me.

I would eventually realize that my mental abilities, intuition and psychic powers were also increasing radically and dramatically, in the same way as my physical powers.

The principles underlying these changes are logical and are well known to us all. Clearly, if one exercises or uses the left side of the body (which is used less often than the right side in right hand dominant people) after years of disuse, one will notice an improvement in right brain function (because the right brain is responsible for left limb function). Similarly, the brain can produce changes in the physical body via neurotransmitters and hormones. A good example of this general idea is the advice given to aging people to brush their teeth with the toothbrush in the left hand, if they have been lifetime right hand brushers. By so doing, it is propounded that the improvement in brain function so generated will be sufficient to stave off dementia!

For more details, you are invited to read Appendix 1 (The Phenomenal and Mysterious Human Brain).

The epiphany of my past existence in 5th century BC Sparta over 2,500 years ago (which had been revealed to me by my immortal spirit-man), gave me a new and exhilarating sense of freedom. I now had a greater insight and understanding of my personal place in the enigma of life, both present and past.

I was in awe of the unique revelation that had resulted from a freak event which would usually kill or maim an individual. The clarity of the memory of my Spartan existence made me feel that it was all part of one life. All the centuries that had passed did not seem to make a difference. It was not as though it was a past and dim memory of something that might have been. It was as real and as significant to me as my present earthly existence.

Chapter 8
Ancient Greek—Modern American

I could now speak fluent 5th century BC Ancient Greek, but I was not about to offer any demonstrations. Revealing this skill would raise too many questions. Before anything else, I needed to grasp the full extent of what had recently manifested in my previously mundane life.

Nevertheless, not all of my past was entirely clear. I seemed to be tapping into some events clearly and distinctly; but, just like a jigsaw puzzle, there were gaps that needed to be filled to make the picture clear. I sensed intuitively that the missing pieces would come to me slowly but surely.

SPIRIT CONTINUUM

There was one thing that I was absolutely sure of beyond any shadow of doubt. An immortal spirit-man, which was now mine, had inhabited another physical body millennia ago and it now resided in my mortal, perishable, physical body called Apollo Rhodes. I had effectively lived that life, but obviously in a different physical body (called Paris Apollo) and I could remember all of that existence, as if I had experienced it in my present physical body.

My soul (my conscious mind, my personality, my emotions, my physical brain and my intellect) by virtue of a freak (perhaps miraculous) accident, now had the capacity to communicate with my spirit-man, on a level previously unheard of. My spirit had lived before in another era of human history and I had the memories to prove it. I knew that I was not delusional. Some might call it reincarnation, but I do not, because that word has connotations and implications which are inappropriate for my situation. I believe that what happened to me is more accurately described as a 'spirit continuum'.

I was a modern American youth and felt honored and privileged to be so. At the same time, I was proud to have been a Spartan warrior and I would always be so. I was beginning to think like an ancient warrior, tempered by the knowledge and zeitgeist of a 21st century western world.

To my knowledge, no-one else has ever been given the unique gift of the revolutionary life-changing knowledge that has been revealed to me as a result of being struck by lightning. (My second episode of loss of consciousness arising out of the mugging served to facilitate the process.)

My life had now taken on new meaning and had far greater dimensions than I could have ever imagined. I now knew with certainty that, although our physical life is precious and should be cherished and valued, death should not be feared, because our immortal spirit lives on forever. It is either housed in a heavenly mansion embraced by the unconditional and limitless love of an omnipotent and omniscient paternal God, or in the body of a human being who the Force for Good can use to express his love and perform his miraculous works in an imperfect physical world.

In fact, the only way that the Almighty Force for Goodness and Love (the Force for Good) can disseminate those eponymous attributes is through his human creations who have been created in his image. But they must be prepared to be his instruments and not be enticed away from his will by the forces of darkness which are ever-present tempters.

ACTS OF GOD

The unpredictable forces of nature can be destructive and cruel. They sometimes show no mercy to young or old, weak or strong, rich or poor, good or bad. They are sometimes incorrectly called 'acts of God', especially by insurance companies.

The spirit of God is not contained in those forces, neither is God's good and beneficent spirit contained in the physical bodies of those who are evil and who violate or perpetrate murder on innocent, helpless children. Such physical bodies are possessed by the evil one—the antithesis of the Good Force!

The exciting and exhilarating aspect of my spirit-man revelation was that I continued to have a strong anticipation that there was still more to be revealed. I knew instinctively via the new-found connection between my brain and my spirit that further revelations were coming, but that they would come in their own way and in their own time.

When I was eventually released from hospital, I actually felt better and stronger than I had ever felt before. I realized how close I had been to leaving my present existence through the attack of those assailants.

I was granted some time off work in order to recuperate from the assault, although I knew myself that it was not necessary. Nevertheless, I thought that this would be a good opportunity to reflect and to assimilate, both intellectually and emotionally, all that had occurred.

In my quiet moments of reflection, I raised the possibility to myself that what I had discovered was too preposterous to believe. After suffering several headaches from thinking too much, I decided that I would try not to analyze what was happening to me, but just accept whatever my spirit-man revealed to me. However, I still relied on my conscious mind or intellect as a guide.

As the weeks passed and I returned to my employment, my desire and zeal for physical development continued unabated and actually escalated. I had been working out at a gym doing resistance and aerobic exercises and people were noticing that I was showing signs of muscular development and aerobic fitness. Nevertheless, knowing that I was, and continued to be, a Spartan gave me an innate and irresistible drive to engage in some form of combative exercises. This was not from feelings of aggression, but merely from a burning desire to hone those skills that I had developed as a warrior so many centuries before in my native Sparta.

CHAPTER 9
MY SPARTAN TRAINING

O ld habits die hard, and I was in a position to take advantage of those good old habits that I had learned as a Spartan. In those days we did engage in boxing and wrestling, as well as discus and javelin. We would lift various sized rocks as part of a weightlifting regime to gain strength. We would also compete against one another with wooden swords and sometimes real swords.

I trained from my early childhood until the day I died. I was taught to endure all manner of hardship and deprivation: to suffer physical pain and even torture without showing any signs of fear or emotion; to survive alone in the extremes of climate; to brave the elements; and to single-handedly hunt animals, small and large, for food, in order to survive. Such was the ethos of the Spartan warrior society.

The uncompromising dedication to physical fitness and training for warfare made the Spartan hoplite (foot soldier) the greatest fighting machine of all time. Those feelings, urges, emotions and impulses kept welling up in my soul and could not be denied, even though I knew that it was the 21st century and that the warrior society of which I'd been an integral part, no longer existed.

I knew in a sense that I was an anachronism, but I also knew that my 21st century American life would temper the ways of my Spartan life in a way which would blend the two cultures harmoniously.

I was starting to regain the strength, size and tone in my arms and legs that I had achieved through endless training and days of battle during the invasion of my homeland in the 5th century BC. It was as though just the thoughts and memories of my Spartan life were having an effect on my physical body. It was for this reason that I felt a strong impulse to seek out a place where I could continue my training. I went looking for a school for self-defense, boxing and martial arts. I found such an establishment, coincidently in an area of the city quite close to where I had been assaulted.

As I walked into the building which housed the Academy of Self-Defense, I was immediately impressed by the state-of-the-art facilities and equipment. However, I experienced a disquieting feeling of unease about it all. As I made enquiries at the reception desk, I noticed three individuals walking about the building. One was a stocky and very muscular Asian man in his late thirties. By virtue of his outfit, he appeared to be a proponent of one or more forms of martial arts (such as wrestling, jujitsu, taekwondo and karate). The smirk on his face projected a friendly, but paradoxically threatening appearance.

Another man of similar age was much slimmer, but with well-developed musculature. He was of medium height with the olive complexion of a southern European or South American. He wore a thick, well-groomed moustache which partially concealed a scar over his upper lip.

The third man appeared to be of African descent being dark skinned. He was very tall, well built and physically imposing. His size and fitness would have qualified him for a job as a bouncer or bodyguard, but he could also have been a useful basketball player.

Despite my intuitive misgivings about the salubrity of this organization, I decided to learn more about it and hopefully hone my physical training and combative skills. Although I was only a novice in the art of self-defense in my present life, I was realizing on a daily basis that my deep-seated and vivid memories as a Spartan warrior were beginning to exert a profound effect on my physical development in the here and now.

I was intrigued by the Academy and enrolled as a member.

With every session that I attended, I could see that I was developing my physical body, my reflexes, my agility and my skills in combat at a rapid rate. I was beginning to be noticed by some of the instructors and some of the experienced students. In the weightlifting sessions, I was able to lift heavier and heavier weights with every passing week.

My muscle definition improved to the extent that other trainees believed that I was using anabolic steroids. This could not have been further from the truth. In fact, I often noticed other trainees furtively using syringes or passing medication bottles to each other. Certainly some of these illicit drug users were also showing signs of massive muscle development, but the growth that they were achieving artificially did not compare with that which I was achieving naturally.

I concluded that my past life memories, which had now become such an integral part of my present life, were initi-ating a remarkable physiological effect on my physical body. In some mysterious way, my memories were causing my brain (hypothalamus) to release hormones which eventually led to an anabolic effect on my body, by a massive outpouring of testosterone to feed my muscles. I was operating on natural steroids that were far more potent than any unnatural exogenous steroids and without the dangerous long-term side effects!

The hormone dopamine, which gives us the power of movement, energy and strength, was flowing into my system whenever I required it. People who use the dangerous drug cocaine experience an increase in dopamine, but they need more and more cocaine to achieve the same level of satisfaction. The dopamine that was available to my system naturally and healthily was far in excess of that which a cocaine addict would need to get high. I was on a natural high, with muscle power and strength whenever the occasion called for it.

Serotonin, the 'feel good' hormone, was also flooding my system in those moments when I needed to relax, remain calm and to focus.

My hypothalamus was also initiating the production of huge amounts of endorphins, the chemical in our bodies which helps us deal with pain and promotes the healing of tissues. People who are addicted to heroin have an artificial form of endorphins, which can never satisfy them and which ultimately causes their self-destruction. Eventually, through constantly relying on an artificial exogenous form of endorphins, ie. heroin, morphine and codeine, they are unable to make their own natural endorphins and must rely on the artificial kind just to remain 'normal'.

I was privileged to be receiving endogenous 'morphine' which is entirely healthy, but it was in far higher proportions in my body than anyone else on the planet. I was therefore able to withstand the pain of trauma in any form, whether it was blunt or sharp, hot or cold.

As a Spartan warrior, I had trained myself by virtue of the nature of my cultural upbringing to withstand and block out pain without showing any emotion. This was befitting a warrior of my race, but now my ability to do so was magnified and enhanced manifoldly, because I was releasing larger and larger amounts of endorphins into my system in response to pain.

Much to my surprise, I also noticed that I was healing a lot faster than I ever had before. Cuts and abrasions, which normally would have taken a week or two to heal, were healing in a matter of hours and sometimes minutes!

Chapter 10
Strange Goings-On

From time to time in the course of frequenting the Academy, my hunger led me to search for suitable restaurants offering a healthy meal. There was a vegetarian restaurant next door to the Academy, but I got the feeling that there was something suspicious about the goings-on in this restaurant. I went back a few times and there seemed to be something unusual about the staff working there. Some of them had a poor understanding of English and I occasionally received the wrong meal. However, rather than make a fuss and embarrass somebody, I accepted what I was served without complaint. In any case, the meals were quite inexpensive.

Another thing that came to my attention was the fact that some of the staff appeared to be glassy eyed and tired. Some of them even looked decidedly ill, based on the pallor of their skin. The other thing that I found curious was the irregularity of the opening hours. The 'closed' sign would often appear at unusual hours of the day and at short notice.

At other times the 'open' sign would be displayed, but there was no-one on hand to offer any service, despite appeals from myself or other potential customers. Nevertheless, there were always at least two people in attendance in the evenings and through to the early hours of the morning, when there were few if any customers at all.

The impression that I gleaned was that they were attempting to discourage customers, by claiming that they had run out of food such as bread and vegetables.

The whole set-up seemed rather suspicious to me. I wondered whether there was something else going on behind the scenes to justify the existence of this poorly run business. My curiosity had been aroused and I was determined to find out what was going on, even though I felt a degree of apprehension about what I might discover.

In the course of my investigation, I surveyed the premises surrounding the Academy and the restaurant. Next door to the restaurant was a large two-story house with a wide frontage, and the building seemed to stretch back quite a distance. This was a semi-detached structure in conjunction with another two-story building, which was also quite large. Next to the latter building was a freestanding commercial building, which was being used as a late-night disco or nightclub.

The nightclub door was open for business, or so it seemed, from about 10pm to 5am. During those hours, the door was always manned by at least two, and sometimes three, large and well-muscled security men or 'bouncers'. The door to the nightclub was actually on the side of the building, as it was on the corner of a lane and the main street.

Interestingly, there were no signs on the outside of the building to indicate that it was a nightclub, but the loud monotonous music emanating from within, combined with the presence of security men, left no doubt that it purported to be a nightclub of sorts. Based on my observations over several weeks, the security men were very selective and discriminating about the clientele they allowed to enter the building.

On one occasion I attempted to gain entry, but was told that it was a very exclusive private club and that there was no way of becoming a member without disclosing all of my credentials. In addition, I was told that acceptance as a member of the club also depended on the recommendation of one specific individual, who provided members with passwords. The identity of the specific individual was not disclosed, but the password, specific to each member, was verifiable. It was evidence that the prospective member of the club had been in contact with the undisclosed authority and was therefore eligible for admission.

This convoluted explanation of the admission process indicated to me that it was not possible to become a member and gain admission. It was indeed a very exclusive club and I could see that it was pointless trying to circumvent the stipulated requirements without arousing more suspicion about my motives for wanting to join.

Next door to the nightclub, there was another two-story building with its frontage in the side street. That building had a driveway which led to a massive garage, big enough to house a large truck and several cars as well. I would often see trucks going up the driveway and into the garage. The trucks were covered so it was not possible to see what they were carrying.

The trucks usually entered the garage late at night but, on one occasion, I was able to glimpse a truck entering the garage. As the truck stopped and the garage door was closing, I briefly saw people coming out of the back of the truck. They seemed to be of all ages, from young to middle-aged, both male and female, and they appeared to be poorly dressed. However, I was unable to make out any fine details.

I did notice a small scrap of paper fall to the ground from the back of the truck, just before it entered the garage. The thin piece of paper must have been pushed through a crack by one of the passengers. I quickly, but furtively, picked up this paper and put it in my pocket in case anyone was observing me. I returned home that evening with the paper, on which were written these words: *please help us*.

Based on the odd goings-on, the people that I had encountered at the Academy, plus the unusual and secretive businesses being conducted close by, I was convinced that there were illegalities afoot. My suspicions were further aroused by the fact that I had almost been killed by assailants near this area. The desperate note plaintively seeking help was the clincher. I concluded that it all needed to be investigated.

Chapter 11
Another Epiphany for Apollo

It was the night of a big boxing, wrestling and martial arts exhibition at the Academy. It was an informal evening with no prizes or titles on the line, but there was a strong sense of pride and competitiveness among the participants. It was an event where those who had been training hard over the previous months and years could demonstrate their talents and progress.

The instructors and the more experienced members of the Academy exhibited their mastery of their chosen form of self-defense before the newer trainees were invited to challenge them in front of a substantial audience of onlookers.

I had dabbled in a bit of boxing over the previous few weeks, but I certainly was not ready to engage in a boxing bout with an experienced pugilist. Nevertheless, I was becoming stronger all the time and my level of fitness and muscle definition were on the rise. My resilience to injury and my ability to heal were also improving week by week. I therefore felt that I had nothing to lose by accepting a challenge to compete.

The man who issued the challenge was the swarthy man with the full moustache which almost covered a scar over his upper lip. He was one of the three characters I had seen on my first day at the Academy. He certainly had the well-conditioned physique of a dedicated boxer in training. Just from his well-defined upper body musculature, it was obvious that he would be a formidable opponent, based on his fitness alone. Whether he had the boxing skills required to match his physique I was about to find out.

We were both required to wear headgear, to comply with health and safety regulations. So I did not feel as though I was taking too much of a risk, despite my previous head injury. As the bout got underway, I tried to display confidence through the use of evasive footwork. He was clearly an experienced boxer and, as I later found out, he had been formerly ranked among the top professional boxers in the world in his weight division. However, I had the advantage of youth and quick recuperative powers.

In the middle of the fourth round, despite my strength and resilience, I somehow lost my footing—there may have been some foul play from outside the ring. As I tripped, my arms dropped and my opponent took the opportunity to land a heavy blow to the left side of my jaw and a quick left hook to the right side of my head. I fell heavily to the canvas. The strength drained out of my body and I lapsed into a state of unconsciousness.

I entered into what initially seemed to be a dream state. A kaleidoscope of images flashed through my brain. The images consisted of various bouts in which I was a contestant, alternating with wrestling, judo and scenes of hand-to-hand combat. As I lingered in this dream state, the images and scenes became more vivid. I then awoke in a cold sweat to find myself in what appeared to be a hospital bed.

I was in a single room, well-lit by bright sunlight streaming gloriously underneath a half-drawn window shade. Through glassy eyes and blurred vision, I looked at a calendar on the wall beside my bed. It read— January, 1944!

Before I had time to think, a tall, well-built, middle-aged man, dressed in the uniform of a US Marine officer of high rank, strutted into the room and addressed me with a degree of frustration in his voice: 'Well Sgt. Power, so you've finally decided to arise out of your state of slumber. It's about time!'

He continued in a stern but avuncular tone, 'We've got a war to win and you go and get yourself knocked out while training raw, wet-behind-the-ears rookies. The nursing staff tell me that you've been hallucinating for the last three days and babbling on in gibberish ... not making much sense at all.'

The officer continued, chuckling facetiously, 'It's just as well you didn't give away any defense secrets, Power, ha ha! The good news is that your medical report indicates that you're going to be okay. Your doctor says you should be fit to get out of here within a week. Then I want you to report to my office. Your confidential orders will be on your office desk by the time you are released from hospital. Speedy recovery and good luck!' He then briskly strode out of the room, leaving me somewhat stunned.

As I sat in my hospital bed, now fully awake, the memory of the events which resulted in my admission to hospital came flooding back to me clearly. As a drill instructor stationed in Pearl Harbor, I had been instructing the new recruits assigned to me in the art of self-defense, using the various types of improvised weaponry that one might find on a battlefield.

Embarrassingly, in an unguarded moment, having turned my attention to another rookie, one of the overly zealous recruits hit me on the head with one of the makeshift weapons and rendered me unconscious. It was the oldest trick in the book—distraction. Divert your enemy's attention from the task at hand and you can overcome him in an unguarded moment.

According to information obtained from the hospital staff, I had been completely unconscious for about twenty-four hours. Then I had been semi-conscious, in a state of delirium, for a further two days. By the fourth day I was responsive to verbal stimuli, but remained drowsy.

Fortunately, I was now more alert and conscious of my surroundings. Consequently, I became more aware of the nursing staff. One attractive young lady in particular caught my eye. Her name was Cassandra, but she preferred to be called Sandra. As my stint in hospital drew to a close, I became more familiar with this young lady and began to develop a strong affection towards her. She seemed to reciprocate my feelings within the bounds of professional etiquette. When it was time for me to leave hospital, she agreed to meet me on her day off as she was unfamiliar with Hawaii and, fortunately for me, knew nobody to show her around.

As the days and weeks passed, it was clear that we were very compatible. We enjoyed doing the same things and we enjoyed each other's company. Men and women since time immemorial have searched for the love and affection of that special one who will provide them with the security of long-term love and friendship.

The blessing of healthy children, as the fruit of their union, has invariably been an important aspiration of couples. Women are particularly committed to this quest as the potential mothers and homemakers of future generations. However, our generation was involved in a world war which created uncertainty about the future and very little predictability.

Until this war was won by the Allies, the life of any man in uniform was not really his own. He was at the beck and call of the military leaders of his country. In effect, I was just a pawn on the chessboard of war. My commanders could position me anywhere they envisaged would be best to achieve the ultimate objective of total and unconditional victory over the enemies of the USA. Sandra and I knew that we could not make long-term plans for our future while the war was still in progress.

By the end of 1944, it was clear that the Allies were gaining the upper hand, both in Europe and in Southeast Asia. The battle of Leyte Gulf (the Philippines) in October 1944 was a decisive victory for the United States over Japan, and it spelled the beginning of the end to Japan's quest for power. But it was appreciated that Japan would never capitulate, as the ethos of the Japanese soldier was to never surrender.

In secret discussions with my superior officers, it was evident that, in order to achieve total and final victory over Japan, untold numbers of American lives would have to be sacrificed. Though in retreat and on the defensive, the Japanese Imperial Army and Navy still constituted a formidable foe and an extremely dangerous opponent.

Of the many islands in the Pacific occupied by the Japanese armed forces, there was one which the US military heads believed was of supreme strategic importance. It had to be controlled by the US, in order to bring about the final defeat of Japan. It was called Iwo Jima. A massive landing of Marines had to be undertaken, in order for the island to be annexed. As a sergeant in the Marine Corps, my role was pivotal. It was, therefore, with great reluctance and a feeling of gloomy apprehension that I called on Sandra— the person who now meant the world to me—to inform her of my mission.

Chapter 12
Semper Fidelis

I had been a loner most of my life, since the death of my parents in a road accident when I was only four. I was raised by a kindly old aunt, but she had long since passed away.

I needed a family, so I joined the United States Marine Corps when I was seventeen. My credo in life had become that of the Marines, namely *Semper Fidelis* or *Semper Fi* for short, meaning 'always faithful'. We lived by the belief that 'once a Marine, always a Marine' which I interpreted as once a family member, always a family member. As a teenager, that gave me the stability I desperately needed.

I was born Peter Power in 1915 and so was in my 29th year when I met Sandra. As a Marine, my life had been very tough and regimented, but it had a sense of purpose. The physical and academic training that I received in the corps had been fulfilling and rewarding. I had swiftly moved to the rank of Sergeant. I had always been interested in hand-to-hand combat and any form of self-defense, including boxing and wrestling. However, my social life had been somewhat dull, as I had given the corps all of my passion and attention. I had never been in hospital before, as I had been fortunate enough to avoid any serious physical injury. So, my meeting Sandra was definitely serendipitous.

In the months that followed our first meeting, I fell deeply in love with her. Although I'd had brief friendships with a few other girls, they had not touched my heart like Sandra. I thought about her day and night. When I woke in the morning, I could not wait for the moment when I would be able to see her, speak to her and caress her. However, my job was demanding and her duties as a nurse were time-consuming.

In the time away from work, when we were able to spend precious moments together, we would sometimes listen to music. We both loved the big band sounds of Tommy Dorsey and Glenn Miller, as well as Frank Sinatra's songs. One of our favorite records was the song by Tommy Dorsey and Frank Sinatra called *This Love of Mine*. We played it when we were together and I also played it when I was alone, because it made me feel that she was still with me. One of our other Frank Sinatra favorites was *I'll Never Smile Again*.

It was February 1945; when I told Sandra that I was going to Iwo Jima, she burst into tears! She could sense, from my tone of voice and demeanor, that it would be a dangerous mission. I felt in my soul that the landing and the battle for the island would be one of the hardest fought and most dangerous encounters in the Pacific for the Marines.

Prior to knowing Sandra, I had less fear of dying. I had fought other battles in the Pacific with calmness and resolve, steadfast in the knowledge that if I had been injured or killed, it would have been in the service of my country. If my life had to be sacrificed, it was for a worthy cause—the preservation of my country's freedom. But now it was different. I had Sandra to live for and I needed to make sure that I stayed alive and returned to her.

I now had someone special that made my life precious to me, because my life was also precious to her. For the first time in my life, I honestly cared more about someone else than I cared for myself. And isn't that the real meaning of true love?

My heart kept telling me not to go into this battle, but my head and all my years of training in the Marines demanded that it was my duty and my obligation. I had to support all those younger and less-experienced recruits who desperately needed the benefit of my military experience and expertise. I couldn't abandon them. I owed it to them, the corps and to my country to be there in the thick of battle with them.

As Sandra and I caressed each other and lovingly embraced on the night before the departure of my unit for Iwo Jima, we both candidly expressed mixed emotions of eternal love and stomach-churning apprehension. I tried to both reassure her and convince myself that victory was certain and that it was just a matter of how long it would take to secure the island.

My words to her were, 'Sandra, don't worry your gorgeous head. This'll be a cakewalk. Our boys will bomb the island into submission long before we set foot on it. Then it'll be just a matter of rooting out the defenders that refuse to surrender. Sure, there's always some danger when you have a stubborn enemy that won't give up—an enemy that wants to take you down with him. But that's what being a fighting Marine is all about.'

'Oh Peter!' Sandra cried, tears streaming down her face, 'I can't bear the thought of anything happening to you. This will be the first time that you've gone into serious combat since we met, and I'm so afraid. Isn't there some way that you can get out of going? The way everyone's talking, it sounds like the war will soon be over. I don't want to lose you now, when the whole thing is so close to finishing.'

'My darling, wonderful Sandra,' I appealed to her, 'if only it were that simple. But you know as well as I do that I'm a professional Marine—it's my chosen career. I can't run away from battles because the risks are high. Look, I promise you, my sweetheart, that I'll be very careful and take as few chances as possible. So, let's enjoy this night together. Let's play our Sinatra records. How about we start with *This Is a Lovely Way to Spend an Evening*?'

As the night wore on, we both tried to relax and danced cheek to cheek to the soft music. Departure time was early the following morning and I had to go. 'It's time for us to get a bit of shut-eye. I've got to return to base. I won't see you now until I get back from Iwo Jima. I won't say goodbye because I'll see you again…soon. Just remember the movie we saw last week with Bogey and Bergman … *Casablanca.* Here's looking at you kid.'

We kissed passionately—longer than usual—secretly dreading that it could be our last. I then departed with a casual salute and a wave, while watching Sandra wipe the tears from her beautiful face. As I reluctantly walked away with my eyes welling up, I could hear her say poignantly, 'I love you Peter … I will always love you. I'll be praying for your safe return.'

CHAPTER 13
THE BATTLE OF IWO JIMA

Months before our arrival, Iwo Jima had been shelled mercilessly from the sea and by air. Such bombing had been repeated for several days before we Marines made our landing. Unfortunately for us, the Japanese had built a network of bombproof shelters and tunnels. On the island there were also caves, which gave the enemy protection and shelter. These factors, combined with the deeply ingrained Japanese ethos of fighting to the death and never surrendering, made our objective of occupying the island an extremely dangerous one.

When we landed on the island, the resistance we encountered was frighteningly ferocious. We suffered many casualties and our death toll was higher than anticipated.

I had to say goodbye to a lot of fine young men in those initial days. I kept thinking of their families and loved ones who would miss them so dearly, but who would never see them again. I was also amazed at the determination of the enemy in their dogged resistance against a foe that they must have known they could not beat.

After many days of heavy fighting, we reached the highest point on the island known as Mount Suribachi. As a symbolic gesture of our virtual victory, I was to join several of my unit in raising old glory on top of the mountain. However, just before that happened, I was taken by a sniper's bullet which penetrated my heart. The sniper revealed himself by the direction of his fire and was quickly dispatched by a rain of bullets from my men.

As my spirit-man left my body, I could see my men standing around me in dismay. Some were weeping openly, while others knelt down with their hands on their heads in anguish and disbelief.

So many young American lives had been lost in this battle already, yet the reverence and outpouring of grief at my loss seemed greater than I had ever witnessed before. Perhaps it was out of respect for my leadership. My second-in-command found my last letter to Sandra in my shirt pocket. I was going to mail it later that day.

Chapter 14
Once a Marine, Always a Marine

As from a vivid, all-consuming, animated dream, Apollo Rhodes awoke suddenly in a lather of sweat in the boxing ring. His heart was pounding. It felt to him as though he had been dreaming for a lengthy period of time, but less than ten seconds had passed since he had hit the deck. In the realm of the spirit, time is meaningless.

Just before the count of ten, Apollo rose to his feet from the canvas, mumbling to himself *semper fidelis* and *once a Marine, always a Marine*. He was now empowered with all the experience and training that made him a champion boxer and martial arts exponent as a Marine during World War Two. He was also imbued with the courage, determination and indomitable spirit of a battle-hardened Marine veteran. Armed with such finely honed fighting skills and assets, Apollo easily disposed of his adversary, who was astonished and frustrated to be beaten by a relative novice.

In the crowd gathered to see the demonstrations of the various martial arts was the man who had nearly put a bullet in the head of Apollo. He had acquired the epithet of 'Mr. Big', either for his girth or his elevated position in the hierarchy of crime. He was flanked by two physically well-built and imposing men, who presumably were the security entourage for the out-of-condition and rotund Mr. Big.

One of the bodyguards was known as 'the Doc'. I later learned that he had once dabbled in nursing and was renowned for his use of injections, often administered for dubious reasons. The other carried the appellation of 'the Ape', because of his thickset body habitus, long arms and stooped posture.

With a quizzical look on his face Mr. Big queried, 'Isn't that the boy we found snooping around the neighborhood? I would have put paid to him had it not been for the arrival of those police cars.'

The Doc interjected, 'Hey, I'm damned if I didn't see that guy snoopin' around when the trucks came in last night. He's too nosey for my liking. I'm sure he's up to no good.'

'Yeh, I know what you're thinking, Doc. He needs to be eliminated and we'll do it in the same way as we did with the others—no traces!' Mr. Big laughed sardonically, as he recalled the two FBI agents who had 'accidentally' disappeared. The FBI had classified their disappearance as 'mysterious', as their bodies had never been found.

Although those two murdered men had been confirmed to be agents, no evidence had been found in Apollo's briefcase that in any way connected him to any investigative, intelligence or police organization. The malevolent Mr. Big and his band of followers had murdered, on suspicion, any strangers who had the misfortune to stray into their territory.

Mr. Big directed Doc and Ape to tail Apollo as he left the building. They were told to follow him home and to look for any information they could gather about him. If in that process Apollo were to have an unfortunate accident detrimental to his health—then so be it.

The deadly duo pursued Apollo to his home and then subdued him at gunpoint. While gagged and bound, Apollo was given an injection intended to put him into a deep sleep and ultimately cause his death. In his powerless state, Apollo was placed in the back of a vehicle and transported to a remote uninhabited area in the country.

That area was known to be inhabited by packs of wolf-like dogs or coyotes, as well as venomous snakes. Sightings of mountain lions and black bears had also been reported.

Their devious criminal minds led them to the conclusion that by dumping Apollo's body in such a location it was never likely to be found. Even if it were discovered and an autopsy performed, there would be no scientific way of determining the cause of death. There were no gunshot wounds, knife wounds or any sign of trauma linking his death to human involvement. The lethal injection was of a type that would be undetectable and there would be nothing to support an act of violence.

If he were to be devoured by scavenging animals, then there would be no trace of his body apart from disintegrating bones. Even so, the vultures would likely consume those. On the other hand, had he been buried alive in a grave too deep for animals to dig up, his body could be exhumed and his identity verified.

This was the perfect crime: no body, no clues and no connection to any group or person. Who knows how many FBI agents had been lost in the same way? But this time Mr. Big's henchmen had picked on the wrong guy!

Chapter 15
Another Side to Apollo

As he lay motionless in his paralyzed state from the effect of the drug that had been injected into him, Apollo continued to breathe in oxygen through the thin layer of leaves that gathered over his body. In this state, he would probably have been missed by a hiker walking past, but the smell of his body would have been easily detected by a scavenging animal in the vicinity. In a typical man of his age and size, the effects of the drug would have caused the body to shut down and die by now; but Apollo's body was different—and so were his mind, spirit and soul.

Since the lightning bolt accident, the changes that had occurred in Apollo (physically, physiologically, mentally and spiritually) had been phenomenal and ongoing. Although the drug had induced a deep state of sleep, similar to a general anesthetic, his respiratory muscles and his strong heart muscle had not been affected. The skeletal muscles of his arms, legs and abdomen had been temporarily inactivated, so that he was unable to move. Apollo was, therefore, effectively paralyzed. However, his magnificently supercharged brain and nervous system, aided by his magnified recuperative powers, were now focused on neutralizing the unwanted chemicals that had been injected into him. Apollo's remarkable liver and kidneys were also working overtime to metabolize and excrete the harmful poison from his body in a manner and rate unequaled by any living person.

During the many hours of his semi-comatose state under the influence of the injected drug, Apollo's spirit-man again rose out of his physical body. As his spirit became free of his body, the memory of a past existence started to emerge by virtue of his enhanced brain and neuronal connections, as well as major improvements to his DNA. He was tapping into the revelations from his freed spirit, which had experienced past events albeit in a different body.

The physical body perishes and turns to dust, but the soul and spirit of a man are eternal and immortal. The spirit remembers well, but I dare say that none but Apollo had the brain to receive information from the spirit. Those memories were initially brief, hazy and fleeting, but they gradually became clearer.

The year was 1784. I was Pierre Apollinaire, a young man in my early teens. I appeared to be in France. I was speaking German, but could also speak and understand French. A convention was being held in Paris where many great minds had gathered. I was apprenticed to the man whose theory of animal magnetism was being judged by a panel of learned men, under the auspices of none other than King Louis XVI of France. It was, in fact, a Royal Commission.

The identities of the men gathered for this convention may not have been entirely clear to me at the time. However, with the collective knowledge of hindsight, I am certain that those present included Wolfgang Amadeus Mozart, Benjamin Franklin and the great French scientist (generally regarded as the father of modern chemistry), Antoine Lavoisier. The man

I worked for, and whose practice of animal magnetism (later to be known as mesmerism) was being scrutinized, was Franz Anton Mesmer.

In the final analysis, the consensus of the commissioners was against declaring Mesmer's practice of animal magnetism to be 'scientifically proven'. That judgment, however, was based on a lack of knowledge and understanding. There was, and to this day there remains, a great deal of skepticism about matters which cannot be proven, but must be experienced subjectively, in a personal way, like faith.

Nevertheless, there was general agreement that Mesmer had certainly helped a great many people with healings (or had at least improved their physical and mental health) by means which defied explanation. In no way was he condemned for his work but, on the contrary, he was praised by the majority. Indeed, I learned a great deal from Mesmer in my formative years, as I traveled with him.

Animal magnetism can be described as a flowing force, like an invisible magnetic field, that connects all living things, both flora and fauna. One disciple of Mesmer described it as *psychodunamos* which, translated literally from the Greek, means 'power of the spirit or the soul'. It exists, but cannot be seen by the human eye. Indeed, it cannot be perceived by any of the five senses. It requires a sixth sense that very few people have discovered in themselves.

Just as any of the five senses cannot be described or understood by someone who has never experienced them, neither can this sixth sense (the portal to animal magnetism) be understood without subjective experience of it. For example, one cannot describe a color to a person who has been blind from birth nor can music be understood by a congenitally deaf person.

For further insights into Mesmer and Animal Magnetism, readers are invited to read Appendix 4.

In my 18thcentury physical existence as Pierre Apollinaire I later qualified as a physician and psychologist in Vienna. I traveled extensively throughout Europe and North America practicing traditional healing and faith healing. Utilizing my knowledge of animal magnetism, I was able to help the poor and the rich alike to heal themselves through the power of their own minds. Better still, if they believed in the Almighty Force for Good that binds and pervades the universe, I could assist them to be cured and restored physically and mentally by the power of their own faith in a benevolent God.

In return for my services, I asked nothing of the poor other than temporary lodgings and to break bread with them if they had food to spare. Of the rich, I expected more and usually received it in abundance, enabling me to continue my work. I was true to my Hippocratic Oath.

Appendix 5 contains the classic version of The Hippocratic Oath.

CHAPTER 16
BACK TO THE PRESENT

Memories of my 18th century life started to dim, as my spirit returned to my physical 21st century body. At the same time, a hissing sound became louder and louder in my ears. As the sound became deafening, I felt a surge of power flow through all the muscles in my body and, as it did, I sat bolt upright in time to see a large snake above my head. Without a moment's thought and with lightning fast reflexes, I grabbed the snake by its neck and flung it with unexpected herculean strength about twenty feet into the air.

Simultaneously, an eagle observing the serpent from its perch in a nearby tree, swooped down and grabbed the snake's head with its talons. The raptor flew skyward with awesome speed and, when it had reached a lofty height, dropped the snake onto a rocky outcrop below, thus delivering the coup-de-grace and ensuring its next meal.

The sun was starting to sink low in the afternoon sky, evidenced by the incipient twilight and the lengthening shadows of the trees. I realized that I had been lying in this spot exposed to the elements for about eighteen hours. No wonder I felt dry in the mouth and very thirsty.

I had no idea where I was, but it certainly looked very rustic and secluded. After some reflection, I determined that, as it would soon be dark and cold, it would be more prudent to make a campfire and find somewhere to shelter for the night rather than look for a highway—if, indeed, one existed nearby.

As I surveyed the area around me looking for kindling wood and a relatively safe place to repose, I reflected on the events of the previous twenty-four hours. My home had been invaded by vicious, ruthless men. They had been ordered by Mr. Big to leave no evidence or signs of physical abuse, in case my corpse were to be discovered by the authorities. However, being sadistic killers, they couldn't resist torturing me with lit cigarettes and knives in an endeavor to extract information from me. They had every intention of killing me, but their methods, in my case, had proven ineffectual. They had transported what they believed was my dying body, by motor vehicle, to an uninhabited area where they assumed my dead body would be consumed by the area's wildlife and never be found.

Fortunately, I was alive; but I was still stranded and dehydrated in a wilderness with no food or water, and with the dark and the cold of night fast approaching.

Prior to the event that transformed my mundane existence and changed my whole perspective on life, death and the afterlife, I would have been terrified and on the verge of tears in this situation. But I was no longer that naive, pusil-lanimous milksop. I was no longer that sheltered, callow youth. I was now a totally metamorphosed man, changed by the experience and knowledge of past lives, which had now become integrated and inextricably linked with my present mortal existence.

I was, at the same time, all of the following:

- an ancient Spartan warrior with elite combative and survival skills and a stoic ability to live in the most austere and deprived conditions.

- a veteran United States Marine, battle hardened and trained to the highest level in martial arts, boxing and self-defense, with an unparalleled esprit-de-corps symbolized by the motto *Semper Fidelis.*

- an 18th century man of learning in medicine, psychology, hypnotherapy and animal magnetism, who had traveled extensively in old-world Europe and the incipient USA, rubbing shoulders with some of the greatest and most famous figures in history.

Chapter 17
Memories of Long Ago

Huddled round the fire that I had started from gathered kindling, I gazed into a night sky devoid of city lights, awestruck by the canopy of effulgent stars above me. As I lifted my head to the sky, I caught a brief glimpse of a shooting star and chuckled to myself, as I recalled what my mother would tell me in Sparta 2500 years ago.

'Paris, my son,' she would explain in a serious voice, 'you and I have just been privileged to witness one of the gods riding through the night sky on their chariot. It may have been Nyx, goddess of the night, or even our patron god, Apollo himself.'

As I sat in vigil over my campfire, a strange calmness descended on me, in a situation which normally would have generated a great deal of angst and terror. I kept reminding myself that I was a new man, with knowledge and experience that no-one else could possibly dream of.

As I added more wood to the fire, I stopped suddenly when I heard the distant sound of howling, either from wolves or coyotes. Wolves had been familiar to me in Sparta, where many wolf packs inhabited the hills surrounding our city.

My paternal Spartan ancestors, were said to have descended from the god Apollo himself. Apart from Ares the god of war, Apollo was our most revered god, mainly for prophecy, athletic prowess and enlightenment. He was also associated with law, philosophy and the arts. We were therefore known as 'Apollonides' and our family name became simply Apollo. These historical facts, or perhaps myths, explain my partiality and respect for the god Apollo. As a Spartan youth I aspired to emulate all of the values he represented and the characteristics for which he was known.

The god Apollo could also be described as a lone wolf. At times he lived with wolves when it suited him. Thus, he understood wolves very well. By the same token, he would not tolerate wolves behaving badly by taking goats or sheep from his flocks or those of his worshippers.

As a young boy training in Sparta, in what was called the *agoge*, I had to kill a wolf in order to survive and prove myself a warrior. As I grew to manhood, I learned to understand wolves more, until I could almost freely walk among them. I came to understand that attacks on humans only occurred when wolves were ravenously hungry or feared for their young. Although there may be some exceptions, wolves usually do not kill for the sake of killing, as man does. They only kill for the sake of their own survival and that of their young. The same principle applies to most predatory animals.

This firsthand experience from my past, combined with my knowledge of animal magnetism, now made it possible for me to communicate with wolves, as well as dogs and other wild creatures, including birds of all kinds, using a silent psychic language or sixth sense.

Aggression in both animals and humans often arises out of fear that an encounter with an unknown creature, man or beast, may constitute a threat. My psychic language made it clear to animals that I was not in their territory in order to harm them in any way. It also made them aware that they should not regard me as potential prey, because there were other animals and food sources in their territory that would serve them much better.

I now believed that I had the power to home in on and interpret the simple thoughts of animals, including birds and sea creatures. By the same token, I felt sure that I could project my thoughts and suggestions into their brains, using animal magnetism or psychic powers with which I had been gifted. More importantly, in order to implement or utilize my gifted powers, I needed to have the key to tapping into them. From the depths of my soul, I felt sure that this key had been given to me through my 18th century learning and experience. I had a premonition that these powers would soon be tested.

As I reflected on these matters of the past, warmed by the flickering flames before me, I felt relatively secure, with my back pressed against a wall of rock which formed a protective alcove around me. Fortuitously, there was also a rocky ledge above me which formed a convenient roof to protect me from wind and rain. However, I started to feel pangs of thirst and hunger again, but now with a greater intensity.

At this moment, from out of the night sky, came the sound of flapping wings. As I looked up, it appeared to be the eagle that I had seen earlier. In his beak he was carrying the remnants of the snake that I had flung into the air and which he had then killed. With precision, he dropped the snake's carcass into my fire. I sensed that he knew that I was hungry and wanted to feed me the rest of the snake that he could not finish.

The eagle perched on the rocky ledge beside me. After a few minutes, as the snake meat started to sizzle and crackle in the fire, he flew off into the night. As soon as the snake flesh showed signs of being cooked, I was unable to resist eating it. It was certainly good to get some food into my stomach, but I was still very thirsty.

I again heard the sound of canine howling. Although I did not know where I was, I doubted whether there would be any grey wolves or even red ones this close to Washington DC or Virginia. I knew that red wolves had been released into South Carolina some years ago and surmised that they could have migrated north and then bred with coyotes.

Wolves are very secretive animals and it is possible that some had survived in the wild, feeding on rodents and small ungulates. Coyotes are well known to be opportunistic hunters. Coy-wolves, which are the offspring of the mating of wolves and coyotes, are seen as larger wolf-like coyotes or smaller coyote-like wolves. Wildlife observers have been tracking their migration south, into states like Virginia, from breeding sites in the northern states, where wolves are prevalent.

Prior to the year-ago event that transformed my life so completely, I was fearful of dogs and all feral animals. I could not have imagined myself living in the wild and surviving. In fact, I was so used to the creature comforts of 21st century city living that even the thought of camping out was completely unappealing to me and not something I had ever done.

APOLLO RHODES — FROM "ZERO" TO HERO

All of Apollo's past-life experiences, knowledge and training were now combining in a young 21st century American man educated in modern technology and popular culture.

Awsome physical and physiological improvements were still manifesting through amazing changes occurring in his brain(initiated by the lightning bolt).

Apollo was also rapidly evolving into a well-rounded and grounded individual of immense personal integrity and exemplary character.

Above all, Apollo Rhodes was beginning to emerge as a formidable and potentially unstoppable heroic figure for good.

Chapter 18
Death Is Not the End

Not surprisingly, the experiences and events that I now unequivocally knew I had lived and died through had changed me completely. They had made me stronger, more confident and far more capable of dealing with whatever challenges confronted me. My firsthand experience of what lies after we *shuffle off this mortal coil* (to quote Shakespeare's *Hamlet*) now meant that I did not fear death at all. For the vast majority of human beings, it is the fear of the unknown that causes them to dread the thought of death.

Be that as it may, there were two good reasons why my mind and my body still desired to cling tenaciously to this physical earthly life. The first reason was the overwhelming desire to stay physically close to family and loved ones and thus postpone their mourning and bereavement for as long as possible. The second reason was the brain chemistry and physiology of human beings, with their numerous hormonal and enzymatically driven pathways. This predicates that we continue to live, as long as it is conceivable, in this physical existence. In other words, we are programmed to prefer our physical life or existence over any after-death spiritual existence. The tenacity to live and persevere in our world, despite its trials and tribulations, is phenomenally strong. It is beyond measure, no matter what our earthly circumstances.

THE CALL OF THE WILD.

As the howling of coy-wolves grew louder, I could see their eyes glowing in the dark and peering at me. Both wolves and coyotes can be quite audacious and aggressive, especially if driven by hunger. Fortunately, I sensed that these coy-wolves, although quite vociferous with their howling, had recently fed and so were not looking for more prey. Using animal magnetism, I conveyed to them the unambiguous message that they had nothing to fear from me.

Through the mental telepathic transmission of my thoughts, these animals now almost considered me a kindred spirit or one of them. They sensed no fear in me and no threat of harm towards them. Consequently, they exposed themselves, emerging from the cover of the forest into the clearing where I sat next to my fire. The group was comprised of four adults and two cubs, all very docile. They were indeed coy-wolves, judging by their size and appearance. I remembered reading about them in wildlife journals and watching documentaries about them on the National Geographic Channel.

Normally, such creatures would be wary of fire. In my presence, the fire seemed to cause them no concern, although they did not come close to it. They simply sat in a resting position, close enough to expose themselves to the warmth of the fire.

I now felt a strong need to slake my thirst and considered chewing on some leaves, in the hope that they might be succulent and provide some moisture. But I was worried that they might be poisonous. I realized that there would be plenty of moisture in the form of dew on the leaves by morning, so I thought it would be better to wait until then.

Just as I was resigning myself to remaining thirsty for the night, the largest of the coy-wolves, undoubtedly the alpha male, rose up on his four legs, looked at me intently and started walking away from the others. After walking a short distance, he stopped and turned his head around, staring at me, implying that he wanted me to follow. Sensing that he wanted to reveal something to me, I followed him without hesitation. There was a full moon and, with the lifting of some cloud cover, the moonlight illuminated the whole area where I had camped.

About two hundred feet away from my campsite, the canine stopped. Lo and behold, hidden beneath some foliage, there was a gently flowing pool of water which seemed to rise from an underground rock pool. I was ever so grateful to this creature as I lapped up the cool, refreshing water with gusto.

With my thirst fully quenched and feeling much revived, I returned to the safety of my campsite with an extremely satisfied grin on my face, closely followed by my four-legged lifesaver. I once again settled into the safety of my rocky alcove, warmed by the blazing fire before me. At that moment, surrounded by these wild, yet friendly, creatures, I felt as though my soul and Mother Nature had united as one.

Being so relieved by what had just taken place, an extreme calmness descended on me. As I watched my canine friends resting before me, my eyelids grew heavy, and I slowly drifted into a sound and peaceful sleep.

CHAPTER 19
SURVIVAL IN THE WILD

As the first rays of the rising sun spread their fiery glow on the horizon, heralding the dawn of a new day, my eyelids flickered open to reveal the dying embers of my now defunct camp-fire. I discovered that my canine friends had departed, but not without first leaving small rounded remnants of their former presence behind them, as animals are wont to do.

I felt cold and again thirsty, yet somewhat rejuvenated by my restful sleep. After relieving myself under the cover of nearby bushes, I wandered down to the spring that I had discovered the night before, to again slake my thirst. I drank as much as was humanly possible, in order to prepare myself for the prospect of a long trek out of this wilderness.

Relying on past-life experience, I knew that the direction of the sun and the direction of the flight of birds would assist me in finding my way to safety. Clearly, I would need to travel eastward in order to reach the Potomac River. This strategy led me through very thickly forested terrain.

After a few hours of trekking, I again felt the pangs of hunger and thirst. I stopped to rest for a few minutes and, as I did, I noticed that the bushes ahead of me were shaking intermittently. I was a relatively safe distance away, and I remained silent and still in order to determine what sort of animal was causing this. After a few minutes, a large black bear and her two cubs emerged from the bushes. Mother bear seemed to be feeding on berries and other types of foliage and her cubs were following her lead. I knew that bears of any kind could be aggressive and dangerous to humans, especially if the bears were accompanied by their young. As before with the coy-wolves, I remained calm and passive, while projecting mental vibrations of peace and universal cooperation through animal magnetism.

Bears are well known for their remarkably keen sense of smell, which has been said to be superior even to that of bloodhounds. So it was obvious to the bear that I was in the vicinity. I could sense that the bear was aware of me, but at the same time I knew that she had also received my cosmic message of goodwill. I was therefore unafraid, but remained motionless even as she slowly approached me. Any sudden movements, especially the act of running, can spark a reflex reaction in a bear to attack.

Much to my delight the adult bear actually started to lick my hand. Was she sampling a taste before eating me or just being affectionate? I knew it was the latter, because I perceived that the mother and her cubs had fed well and that she was not looking for any animal protein. The trio eventually lumbered away, but not before looking back towards me for an affectionate 'bear goodbye'.

As the bears disappeared from sight, I took the opportunity to pick some of the berries and edible flowers that they had courteously left behind on the bushes. I knew that I needed to eat in order to keep up my strength. At the same time, the berries offered me some moisture for rehydration.

CHAPTER 20
THE RAVENS AND
THE MOUNTAIN LION

As I continued on my journey back to civilization, I was struck by the presence of a pair of black birds with shiny plumage that appeared to be escorting me. The two ravens flittered from the ground to tree branches, back and forth, while moving forward, impressing on me the need to follow them. One appeared to have a coin in its beak, the other a ring. Ravens and crows are well known as collectors of jewelry and other glossy objects. The objects they were carrying suggested that there could be people close by.

Ravens are generally regarded by ornithologists and other wildlife experts as the most intelligent of birds, based on studies in captivity where they are able to solve problems beyond the capability of other creatures.

As I continued to follow the ravens, I suddenly heard the sound of human cries in the distance. I quickened my step—the screams became louder and more frantic. As I approached the source of the shrieking, I was surprised to see a large feline creature, which could only be described as a mountain lion. It had a tawny coat typical of its breed. This wildcat is hardly ever seen now in the east of the United States, but unconfirmed sightings have been reported. I can now say from firsthand knowledge that they do exist in this neck of the woods.

The mountain lion was about twenty feet away from the mouth of a cave. One or more people appeared to be throwing small stones and rocks from within the cave towards the mountain lion. Both the stones and the screams were clearly an attempt to frighten the big cat away.

Mountain lions are extremely dangerous and deadly. They are stealthy ambush creatures that will attack the neck and head of their prey with both their jaws and their sharp claws, if they can so position their victim. The poor souls under siege by the cat were defending themselves, in the hope that the creature would give up and flee. However, their defensive stand was not working.

In order to assist them, I transmitted a suggestion to the mountain lion, via telepathic communication, that there were some rabbits and small deer in close proximity and that they might serve as a better food source. Consequently, the animal darted away in pursuit of easier prey, leaving the way open for me to assess the terrified occupants of the cave.

As I entered the cave, there was sufficient natural light for me to see a middle-aged man and woman cowering in one corner with a young female in her late teens lying supine on the floor. Fortunately, inside the cave there were small rocks and broken boulders, which they had used to ward off the cougar, at least temporarily. They had also gathered some broken tree branches, which could have been used as fuel for a fire, as well as weapons of self-defense against wild animals.

The teenager appeared to be ill or injured and oblivious to the dire situation that the group was in. The man and woman who hovered over her, were disheveled, exhausted and terrified. They look surprised to see a stranger appear at this time, but they were obviously greatly relieved. After looking at me again, with their hands raised in the air in a prayer-like posture, they faced each other and spoke frantically in a Spanish dialect. At the same time, they gesticulated vigorously towards the opening of the cave, clearly expressing fear that the mountain lion would return.

As they continued to rant in Spanish, I gently placed my hands on their shoulders in an effort to communicate with them. I asked them clearly, 'Do you speak English?' But the man replied, 'No good.'

The couple then continued to speak directly to me in Spanish, but this time in a calmer, more measured manner. In my new life, with all of the revelations from my previous lives, I had come to expect surprises. I was therefore only mildly surprised to discover that I could clearly understand what they were saying, but I was truly astonished when I started to speak to them in Spanish.

I had never learned Spanish at school and I had never understood it, nor attempted to speak it, in this lifetime. As all of the memories and details of my 18th century European life had not yet totally come to me, I was not absolutely sure, but I was beginning to believe that I had spent some time in Spain. My 18th century experience, combined with my now highly receptive brain cells, were the only logical explanations for my sudden fluency in Spanish.

Although they were speaking in a Central or South American dialect of Spanish, I could certainly communicate with them with my own orthodox Spanish and I understood what they were trying to convey to me.

Now that there was no language barrier, I firstly reassured them that they no longer had anything to fear from the mountain lion nor any other wild creatures while I was with them. Although their facial expressions communicated a degree of disbelief, their body language indicated that they were starting to relax to some extent. I sensed that they were curious about my identity and how I had come to be there. Nevertheless, it was more urgent to ensure that the teenage girl's physical health be stabilized. They explained that she was their seventeen-year-old daughter, Isabella.

It appeared that they had been wandering aimlessly for the last three days, unable to find their way out of the wilderness. They had started off with two small canteens of water, but the supply had been depleted after the first day. They had not been able to carry any food with them.

In her extreme hunger, Isabella had eaten some wild berries. These were obviously poisonous because, sometime after consuming them, she fell ill with crampy abdominal pain, vomiting and diarrhea. Clearly, the diarrhea and vomiting had depleted her of essential bodily fluids and electrolytes. Without adequate amounts of water, her worsening dehydration would lead to kidney failure and death. It was vitally important for her survival that Isabella drink water as soon as possible.

Finding water had now become a matter of life and death. As I strode out of the cave, I looked up to the sky above, offering a silent prayer for divine guidance in my urgent search for water. I quickly scanned the surrounding area looking for any clues. I noticed a large flowering bush, which seemed to be flourishing more than surrounding plants. I also saw a considerable colony of ants nearby and a number of small birds fluttering near the bush. These were signs that there was underground water in this location.

I started to dig into the ground surrounding the well-nourished plant with broken tree branches as fast and as vigorously as I could. The deeper I dug, the softer the soil became. Eventually, a slow but steady pool of water rose out of the ground, indicating the presence of an underwater spring. With no implements or pots available to boil the water, we had to trust in its purity. Fortunately, the water looked clear, so it was a matter of getting Isabella to drink enough to rehydrate her. We all shared the water and, over the course of the next day, the young girl steadily improved until she was strong enough to stand and walk.

During that day, I learned from Antonio and Carmen, the parents of Isabella, how they had become lost in the wilderness. With his faithful wife listening to the conversation and only too ready to contribute to the narrative at any time, Antonio proceeded to tell their story from the beginning.

My English translation is as follows: 'We are very poor farmers from South America. For many years, we barely survived as honest growers of vegetables and fruit. One day, men dressed in fine suits and driving fancy cars came to us and told us they would give us more money to grow this plant called... marijuana.

'My wife and I are not educated people. We know nothing of the laws or rules of government; we only hear what the priest tells us from our holy book. We do not kill; we do not steal, and we do no harm to anyone. All we ask is that God helps us to survive and to lead a life without trouble.

'We welcomed the idea of a bit more money. We would be able to give our children—our son and daughter—an education, so that they could learn and understand the things of the world and have a better life than we have had.

'We see no harm in planting and harvesting. If something can be grown, then it must be God's will for the seeds to be planted. We do not think we are doing anything wrong. These men pay us a little bit more for the marijuana than we would make for selling our vegetables. So, we keep the vegetables for our daily needs—at least we do not starve.

'After a year or so, those same men came to us to say that the federal police may be coming to inspect our area in the near future. They said that the police might arrest us and put us in jail, if they were to discover any evidence of a marijuana plantation. Being simple peasant farmers, we did not fully understand, but we were fearful of going to jail. What would become of our children? Who would take care of them? Would we ever see them again? These questions and more, we asked ourselves, in our state of confusion and panic.

'On the following day, these men returned with a very rich-looking American man. They translated the American's words and led us to believe that, through the generosity of the American government and its people, we and our children had a chance to migrate to the United States, the land of opportunity, at no expense to ourselves. However, this was conditional on our performing certain "simple" duties during our transit to the United States and on arrival. At this point, we were prepared to agree to anything, in order to avoid falling foul of the law in our country. We had heard about the good life in the USA, and we were hopeful for our children at least.'

Listening to poor Antonio's story, I could see what these evil men had perpetrated. Taking advantage of the ignorance of decent, simple people of the land, they were illegally enriching their own lives at the cost of destroying the lives of honest, but gullible, South American farmers. They unconscionably manipulated these ingenuous, uneducated peasant farmers into doing their own bidding, when their backs were to the wall.

Antonio continued his narrative: 'Several days later, after accepting their offer and agreeing to cooperate, my family and I gathered together what belongings we had and were picked up by a big bus and transported to a secluded seaport. We were directed to board a large ship with other passengers and did so with naive optimism. The conditions and facilities on board the ship were very basic. But we were used to living a simple life without luxuries, so we were able to cope.

'During the course of the voyage, our ship stopped at a number of ports, but I had no idea where we were. We were not given any information about the locations, but I did notice that at each port large containers were loaded onto the ship.

After several days of sailing, our ship anchored out to sea. From the ship, we saw the coastline and were informed that we had reached the coast of the United States. Each of us, including many other passengers, were given lifejackets. They were very bulky and heavy. We were instructed to attach them to our upper bodies.

'In groups of twelve, we boarded several speed boats, which had come from the shoreline to meet the ship. The motorboats were navigated at high speed towards the dock. We were then assisted out of the boats and ushered into several covered trucks, still wearing our lifejackets. The trucks seemed to take different routes, but eventually arrived at the same destination about ten minutes apart. All of the trucks entered a massive garage, and we were told to get out. We were then directed to a large courtyard and relieved of our lifejackets.

'In the days that followed, we were assigned different tasks within a massive complex of interconnected buildings. My wife and daughter were given domestic duties to perform.'

By this point in Antonio's narrative, the story was becoming clear. These poor unsuspecting South American farmers were being manipulated into doing the bidding, unwittingly, of people who I suspect were part of a large organization or cartel. The life-jackets probably contained drugs of some kind, judging by the description of their bulkiness.

As he continued his story, it became apparent that Antonio and his 21-year-old son, Fernando, were being forced to farm marijuana, somewhere between six and seven hours away by truck. That farm was isolated and camouflaged to avoid detection from patrolling helicopters. From Antonio's description, it was a huge complex, comprised of many different levels and always guarded by rifle-wielding men in uniforms. Antonio described how the marijuana plants were located outside the complex, but covered by netting. This allowed sunshine to penetrate, but kept the operation concealed. However, I could not understand the purpose for the rest of the complex, with its many levels. Nor was it clear why there were uniformed guards carrying weapons.

Carmen then interjected and explained that while Antonio and Fernando were away in the country for five days per week, she and her daughter Isabella were kept very busy at the city complex. They were assigned tasks by a female supervisor who, from Carmen's description, was a tough, hard-boiled, middle-aged woman lacking in social graces. They were assigned housekeeping and cleaning duties. They also worked in three kitchens, one of which, based on its size, was probably attached to a cafe or restaurant.

Carmen also explained that she and her daughter had witnessed strange goings-on in the complex during the twelve months that they had been in the USA. They would often see men, young and old, coming and going—this was mainly at night, but also in the early hours of the morning. They would be ushered into rooms occupied by very young to middle-aged women, who were scantily dressed and done up to appear more voluptuous and attractive.

They also saw young men exchanging money for paper bags, containing...they knew not what. In addition, there was a single room in the complex which they would often have to clean and that involved the careful removal of needles and syringes. They were told that this was a medical room used by a visiting doctor to treat sick staff members of the organization.

Carmen and Isabella did not really know their geographic location—just that it was somewhere in the US. Antonio and Fernando were similarly in the dark, because when they were being transported by truck to the country, it was always at night and the windows were covered. They were told this was for security reasons.

Carmen and Isabella were also told they could not leave the complex because their immigration papers were still being processed. They were informed that if they were found outside the complex, the immigration process could be jeopardized. Even worse, if their country of origin got to know of their presence in the USA, they could be deported to face a lengthy jail sentence in South America.

These poor, hapless people were obviously bewildered. They were being exploited and blackmailed by veiled threats of serious repercussions, if they did not toe the line and do as they were told. At the same time, they were given the carrot-and-stick treatment. They were assured that if they behaved themselves and were patient, they would receive the security and other benefits of US citizenship.

I was still curious to learn how these three people had wound up in a cave in the wilderness. Antonio explained that the whole family had recently been transported overnight to the large complex in the country. Apparently, they needed two women to assist with cleaning and sundry other duties. As with the complex in the city, this large isolated complex in the country had medical facilities purportedly to cater for the health of managerial staff and workers. There were two large medical rooms, which Carmen and Isabella were required to clean on an almost daily basis. There were many needles, syringes and other medical paraphernalia to be cleaned and then disposed of.

Antonio and Carmen said they saw scientific-looking men and women wearing white coats come and go from a particular area. They may have been doctors, scientists or laboratory technical staff. The male workers at the complex attended the two medical rooms in groups. There was also a third medical area which the girls were not permitted to enter. Most of the medical or scientific staff in white coats came and went from that area. There was a notice on the door stating: *Private—Strictly No Entry.* The staff members would have to swipe a card and apply their thumb print to gain entry.

In the two medical rooms that they were required to clean, the women often saw men taking tablets as they left the room. Some sniffed powder from a little container. Others had band-aid patches or cotton wool balls taped to their upper arms or to the inside of their elbows.

Most of the sharp needles were placed in special disposable containers, which the girls were required to transport to a furnace for incineration. However, sometimes they would find scattered needles which they would carefully pick up with special gloves and place in the waste disposal containers. Even with their lack of scientific knowledge, they knew the danger of used needles.

The family became alarmed when they realized that their son, Fernando, before starting work each day, was also being seen by the 'doctor'. Fernando and his parents had been informed that it was necessary for him to undergo these medical checks and to take certain tablets, so that his health would be optimized before becoming a citizen of the United States. Antonio accepted this initially but, as time passed by, he became concerned about the way Fernando was behaving. His son was having trouble sleeping at night, even after a hard day's work. He became moody, irritable and was constantly sniffing.

Antonio and Carmen also noticed that occasionally Fernando would return from the doctor's office with dressings taped to various parts of his arms, indicating that he had received injections. This was a disturbing development and made them reconsider what was really happening to their family.

The distraught father then told me of an even more confronting and blatant act of human violation. With tears welling in his eyes, Antonio related how two armed security guards had taken turns raping his daughter, while they held him at bay with their guns. He did not actually see what they were doing, but he knew by their actions and his daughter's inconsolable hysteria afterwards that... Isabella had been defiled by the loss of her virginity! Antonio explained that she had remained in a trance-like state for days. Isabella had been reticent to discuss anything to do with her violation, even with her mother.

When Isabella eventually related the sordid details of what had transpired, Antonio was incensed. 'I felt disgust and regret at having brought my family into this situation, where they were vulnerable to the whims of evil and unscrupulous men,' Antonio admitted. 'I determined from that moment that I would do anything to get my family out of this pit of evil that I had unwittingly put them in.'

As they were not permitted to use any communication devices or phones of any kind and were under round-the-clock surveillance, they were virtual prisoners under authoritarian control masquerading as benevolent bureaucracy. The same level of high security and surveillance prevailed in both the city and country complexes. No avenue of escape existed in either place.

Chapter 21
A Bold Escape

It occurred to Antonio and his wife that there might be a slender chance of escaping during transit between the two complexes. It had been decided by the invisible and faceless controllers of the entire project that the family would return to the city on a certain date. Unfortunately, Fernando was required to stay in the country, on the basis that he was not particularly well and would have to undergo further tests and treatment.

So, it turned out that only the parents and daughter were transported by truck under the cover of darkness. Other victims of this exploitation were also being transported, but talking among themselves was discouraged by the driver and his assistant front-seat passenger. Usually the back of the truck was locked throughout the journey. In his heightened state of vigilance, Antonio realized that the duo had forgotten to relock it, after a mid-journey stopover to answer the call of nature. When this opportunity presented itself, Antonio decided that it was time to make an escape.

In order to avoid detection by the police or other government authorities, the journey always involved backroads not commonly used by other drivers. So they were travelling through virtual wilderness areas. There were no lights, signs or paved roads.

When the truck slowed to a virtual standstill, the trio jumped silently from the back door and rushed into the dense woodland surrounding them, not knowing where they were or what dangers lay in store for them. They only knew that they had to escape and communicate with someone about their plight, irrespective of what repercussions flowed from being identified as illegal aliens. Antonio and Carmen realized that they had already exposed their children to far too much danger. Regardless of what happened to them, Antonio and Carmen were determined to prevent their children from being subjected to any further harm.

By the time the two drivers realized that there were three people missing, it was pointless for them to give pursuit. It was too dark and the forest was too dense and impenetrable. It was surmised that the escapees would not survive very long and would eventually succumb to the elements or be devoured by feral animals. So for three days, this desolate trio had wandered around in circles, bereft of food and with only a scanty supply of water. I shuddered to think that had it not been for our fortuitous meeting, the prediction of their drivers about their demise may well have come true.

Although Isabella was now showing definite signs of recovery from her food poisoning and dehydration, another day had elapsed. These people had been lost in the wild for four days, while I had been left for dead about two days ago. I had eaten and, with my resilient recuperative powers, felt very strong. All three of them, although mobile, looked very weak and tired. They needed some food to restore their energy and they needed it soon. Some animal protein would serve that purpose.

As I cogitated on the problem, my old friend the eagle suddenly appeared like a breath of fresh air and gently perched with his massive talons on a tree branch close to my head. He stared directly at me, gazing into my eyes with his golden yellow orbs. He gave me the impression that he was intent on reading my thoughts and, as he did, it was almost as though the soul of the eagle and my soul had blended into one through animal magnetism. After a few minutes the eagle flew off, disappearing into the blue with all the grace and phenomenal speed for which his magnificent species is well known.

About an hour later the eagle returned to where we were camped, as I anticipated he would. He gently deposited a life-giving gift at the entrance to the cave. It was a sizeable rabbit, which he had freshly killed. I then instructed Carmen and Isabella to place extra branches on the fire, so we could cook the rabbit without any delay as they were famished. Naturally, I offered a silent hand gesture of deep gratitude to my feathered friend, as he disappeared like a flash into the sky.

After appropriately preparing the rabbit and cooking it to perfection over the open fire, it was ready for consumption. Isabella was still too weak to feed herself, so her mother fed her the tiny, nutritious morsels of meat from which she would hopefully regain her strength. Carmen and Antonio also shared in the long overdue feast, as did I. They ate their meal with gusto and seemed very satisfied at its completion.

Hunger is terribly debilitating and is an enemy of the human spirit. I was reminded of what Napoleon had once said—*an army marches on its stomach*. And so it was that with their bellies full, I could sense a quantum of renewed hope in the eyes of these good people. I could almost detect a smile trying to break through their weary and forlorn faces. However, Isabella was still too weak to travel.

As the shadows were lengthening and the sun commencing its descent in the western sky, I knew that it was time to camp for the night. The family members needed to renew their strength for the journey next morning. I would keep the fire burning at the entrance of the cave for their warmth and comfort. Even though I was totally confident (thanks to my rediscovered powers of animal magnetism) that we would have no problems with wildlife, the fire also helped them feel more secure about the threat of feral animals.

Although somewhat fatigued myself, I found that with my burgeoning mental and physical strength I required less sleep than the average individual. So, after observing my newly adopted family in a state of restful slumber, I decided to take a walk to breathe in the crisp night air.

The moon was full and the sky cloudless once again. Combined with the golden lunar orb, the canopy of countless stellar lights made it easy to see the nocturnal world of the forest. As my gaze wandered towards the treetops, I was delighted to spot one of my favorite flying creatures of the night—the owl. He had just caught a field mouse and was in the process of devouring it whole, with alacrity. With his stomach full, he too seemed satisfied.

As I stared at the owl, he returned my gaze with equal intensity. He winked at me with his right eye and gave a hoot. With that gesture I could almost hear him say, 'Hi, human friend.' His bright yellow irises loomed large and imposing against the background of the dark shadows of the treetops.

At that moment it became clear to me that the oft-used epithet *the wise old owl* had a basis in fact. This wonderful nocturnal bird of prey was talking to me telepathically and, for the first time, I was experiencing my ability to tap into his brainwaves. The owl understood that I was looking for the most direct passage out of the forest. He sensed that I was concerned about my fellow human creatures, as he had been observing us over the previous days.

In response to my telepathic (magnetic) vibrations of concern, the owl advised me to, 'Look to the ravens and follow their path'. With that, the owl gave me another wink and a vocal goodbye. It was time for him to fly off to swoop down on another unsuspecting mouse. Looking at the stars and knowing that we had to go in an easterly direction, I was confident that I could lead my small party back to the city. Nevertheless, some help from the ravens would indeed be very welcome.

CHAPTER 22
OUT OF THE WOODS

As dawn broke on the following day, I awoke from a revitalizing sleep to find a trio of ravens perched on the branch where the owl had been the night before. I realized that two of them were the ravens that had been carrying the ring and the coin, but they were now accompanied by a friend. They were squawking and flapping their wings, clearly eager to assist me in my journey back to civilization.

In response to the persistent calls of my raven friends, I quickly roused the family from their slumber. Greatly refreshed after their long sleep, the group responded briskly to my exhortations to decamp. Isabella appeared to be remarkably improved, physically and emotionally. The food and the rest had done her the world of good. Her parents also looked rejuvenated and keen to get back to civilization.

As an employee of the United States government, I had explained to the family that I could be their advocate. Once we all returned to the city, I would explain to the authorities responsible for migrants that these people had been tricked and virtually kidnapped by unscrupulous men purporting to represent the government. With that reassurance, the family were eager to return to civilization, so they could be vindicated and absolved of any wrongdoing. They were looking forward to the prospect of becoming free citizens of a nurturing and democratic country.

They were prepared to submit to the authorities and accept whatever consequences flowed. That had to be better than living under a despotic regime, enforced by disingenuous bureaucrats, prison guards, rapists and fiendish pseudo-doctors. Antonio and Carmen were hopeful that Fernando and Isabella would have a new life with prospects of a bright future as United States citizens.

At this time, the family's most pressing concern was to ensure that Fernando be restored to good health. They suspected that he was being used experimentally to test the effects of mind-altering drugs. It was imperative that Fernando be removed from the evil clutches of the organization that was dangerously risking his health and that of many others. It was also exigent that I get back to civilization, in order to expose the men who had attempted to murder me.

With a sense of urgency, we proceeded in an easterly direction, assisted by the ravens. After trekking for nearly the whole day, we reached a public highway and managed to hitch a ride on the back of a truck heading towards Washington DC. Unbeknown to his family, while they had been lost in the wilderness, Fernando had been transported to the city complex, again on the pretext of medical reasons.

As soon as they became aware of Fernando's relocation, a plan was devised by me and agreed to by the family. As the family knew the ins and outs of the city complex, it was agreed that they would lead me inside, despite the risk of them being recognized as fugitives. The family was confident that they could find and rescue Fernando before they were identified as the escapees from the truck.

Once they had rescued their son, the plan was for me to take them to the appropriate authorities to whom they would divulge information on this illegal operation. The hope was that they would be pardoned by the US government, by giving evidence that would help to convict the felons. I would submit that they were deceived into coming to the USA, believing that they were entering the country legally.

Chapter 23
The Evil House of Addiction

When the family arrived at the city complex they were devastated to discover that Fernando's health was even worse than when they had last seen him at the country complex. I could see that Fernando was having difficulty breathing. He was blue in the lips, evidencing a lack of oxygen, and he was laboring to breathe. It was now apparent that Fernando had become a heroin addict and a cocaine user.

It subsequently came to light that other drugs were also administered, with less than gentle persuasion, to make the workers drug dependent. Most drug addicts will do anything to ensure that they're getting their fixes. They become slaves to the drugs and, in turn, become slaves to the drug organization. In this way, a legion of willing and obedient workers is established. Such workers are glad to be paid in drugs which have been imported or manufactured by the organization itself. If some of the workers were to overdose on the drugs and die, or to become too ill to work, there were many more to take their place. Those who were unfit for work became a liability to the organization and were summarily disposed of.

SYNTHETIC MARIJUANA

There was also a synthetic form of cannabis (K-2 or Spice) which made the addicted person all but sell their soul in order to get more. This drug similarly created obedient, willing workers at the mercy of the organization which made a fortune from the sale of illicit drugs.

In a state of disbelief, Antonio expressed horror at the sight of his son with a syringe hanging out of his arm. 'My sick son is worse than ever!' he cried. 'What have these *bastardos* done to my poor boy? They have turned him into a drug addict, with no will of his own. I foolishly believed that these people were trying to help him. How stupid was I? Mr. Apollo, please do not let my boy die. No parent should ever have to bury their child, but I fear that it may be too late for Fernando. I blame myself for what has happened to him. I was so *ignorante* to have been fooled by those unscrupulous men. I swear, by the God of my fathers, that they will pay for this. Please, Mr. Apollo, tell me ... is he dying; is my son dying? Can he be saved? Please tell me you can save him, Mr. Apollo!'

Antonio continued in this hysterical state without abatement, fearing the worst for his son. With words of encouragement, I replied emphatically: 'Antonio, I swear by my forefathers and the ancient gods of Olympus that your son will not die in this way. I call upon the power of the almighty Force for Good to spare your beloved son at this time. Antonio, your powers of comprehension will not permit you to accept this. So, I am going to spare you the dilemma of trying to understand what I am about to say, by talking in the ancient language of my Spartan ancestors.' Speaking in ancient Greek, I then declared: 'I have risked my own life to save young men on the battlefields of ancient Greece and the islands of the South Pacific and I have succeeded. I swear, by all that is holy, I'm not about to let your son die now.'

Fernando was lapsing into unconsciousness, as his muscles of respiration began to fail. He was about to enter a state of respiratory arrest, which would have proved fatal, unless reversed. With all speed, I extracted the needle from his arm.

Then I remembered that there was an injection to neutralize the effect of heroin. I ran down the corridor, looking for a doctor or anyone in a white coat. I grabbed one such individual, screaming frantically, 'In that room, there is a man dying from a heroin overdose; surely you have supplies of a neutralizing injection! I've just remembered that it's called *naloxone*. In the name of humanity, get some! Quickly, get it now or you might be deemed by law to be an accessory in the death of an innocent young man.'

With a look of dread on his face, the man in the white coat rushed into the room where Fernando lay motionless. He scrambled towards a medicine cupboard and found *naloxone*. The man handed it to me saying that he was not a doctor, but that he was sure that this was the 'right stuff'. He said he had previously assisted doctors with similar episodes, adding that such happenings were not uncommon.

He suggested that I jab the *naloxone* into the victim's arm before it was too late. 'I have seen the doctors using this, but I'm only an assistant,' the shaking man explained.

Soon after the injection, Fernando began to show signs of regaining consciousness and his father breathed a huge sigh of relief.

A 911 ambulance was called to the complex and I contacted Prof. Sandberg to ask if his hospital could accommodate

Fernando and take care of him until he recovered. The local police and the FBI were summoned because there were clear signs of illegal drug use on the premises. There were also suspicious signs of child exploitation.

Fernando was ferried to hospital in the presence of his parents and sister. Prof. Sandberg undertook to take care of them in the hospital complex until Fernando recovered.

CHAPTER 24
IS THE JIG UP?

In the meantime, the FBI began investigating the complex where Fernando was found, but many of the people that they questioned were drug addicted. Then a notice was given to unsuspecting employees, informing them that the directors of the Academy of Self-Defense were temporarily closing the Academy in order to conduct repairs and perform other jobs. A sign was placed on the door of the adjoining vegetarian restaurant, stating: *Closed Until Further Notice*. A similar sign appeared on the door of the nightclub.

Having gained entry to the entire complex and having seen for myself what was happening behind closed doors, combined with the information provided earlier by Antonio and his family, I was now able to put the pieces together.

In the commotion surrounding the rescue of Fernando from a drug-induced death, I had seen a number of people scurrying about in the vicinity. I recognized the Doc and Ape who believed they had killed me. I wondered whether they may not also have been instrumental in the near-death incident of Fernando.

I also recognized Mr. Big. He had almost put a bullet in my head when I had been knocked unconscious by the gang of youths. My spirit had floated above my unconscious body enabling me to identify him.

I spotted these three men hurrying to the roof of the complex, which I later learned housed a helicopter pad. However, at that time I was more concerned about saving Fernando than pursuing the miscreants.

Clearly, the intervention of the FBI had sent everyone flying or fleeing. However the federal police, with the help of local authorities, rounded up all of the occupants of the complex for questioning.

Despite all of the damning circumstantial evidence, Mr. Big and his cohorts were able to offer explanations that satisfied the police of their innocence, at least for the present. It may also have been that some of the local police were taking bribes to turn a blind eye.

The gist of the evidence outlined in the police report was as follows:

Some minimum security federal prison inmates, almost at the point of parole or release, had been seconded through federal agencies, such as the National Park Service and the US Forest Service, to carry out labor-intensive work in specialized areas designated by the Federal Bureau of Prisons, which is a branch of the US Department of Justice.

Mr. Big (real name withheld) was high up in the Federal Bureau of Prisons. Some years previously, he had been given the responsibility of finding a suitable location in West Virginia for the construction of a minimum security correctional center. The minimum security prisoners were to be involved in the day-to-day internal running of the center, under the super-vision of correctional officers.

The inmates were also to be employed in a comprehensive program of farming in a designated area around the complex. They were to be allowed relative freedom to carry out their work, under the guidance of professional horticulturalists. However, they were also to be under the ever-watchful eyes of the correctional staff, both within and around the perimeter of the complex. Beyond this perimeter was densely wooded wilderness with an array of wildlife.

Mr. Big had a central office in Washington DC at the US Department of Justice building. He also had a peripheral office, which he attended more frequently. This was situated close to the docks of Washington DC. The peripheral office was located within the complex comprised of the physical culture center, the restaurant and nightclub. His office was on the top floor and was almost impregnable, such was the level of security that he had arranged. Just above his office was the helicopter pad, which he used as his entry point to the building.

Workers in the city complex were the lowest security convicts, who were at the point of re-entry into civilian life. They were trusted to a high degree, but were still kept under the watchful eye of prison bureau staff. Those convicts were referred to as parolees. Their employment involved working in the gym as trainers, instructors, helpers, janitors and cleaners.

In the dormitories, females were employed as house-keepers and cleaners. In the restaurant, both men and women parolees were employed as cooks, kitchen hands, dishwashers, waiters and waitresses. The reason given for children or teenagers within the complex was that they were family members of the parolees. They were invited to spend time with the convicted family member, in order to facilitate their healthy reintroduction into society on leaving prison.

Another justification for the presence of juveniles was that they were young offenders, being trained to live harmoniously in a social community setting. Presumably, they had no healthy family life to which they could return.

The explanation for non-English speaking men and women within the complex was that they were illegal aliens awaiting evaluation and processing, before a decision was made by the Department of Immigration as to whether they could stay or be deported.

The justification for the medical examination and injecting rooms and for the supply of heroin was that some of the inmates were opiate (heroin) drug addicts. It was considered prudent that they be given the drugs under supervision in diminishing doses, so they could actually be weaned off the practice of injecting. They were also given oral methadone or buprenorphine as a substitute for heroin.

The explanation for the late-night liaisons by men at the center was to do with the provision of therapeutic massage, which formed part of a holistic approach in the treatment of stress, chronic pain and drug addiction. It was claimed to be a substitute for habit-forming, over-the-counter pharmacy drugs and, even worse—illicit, addictive drugs.

In the light of the above statements of clarification, it was argued that there was sufficient evidence of propriety for what was happening at the complex. However, lots of little things were hard to explain and raised doubts as to the legality of the whole organization.

In order to prove any illegal wrongdoing on the part of this organization, the testimonial evidence of people 'in the know' was required. Such people were those who were directly involved in the day-to-day running of the organization. Evidence had to be given by Antonio and his family and others who had been exploited and harmed. Mysteriously, such people (not to mention FBI investigators) had a tendency to go missing before they could provide any incriminating evidence.

I reasoned that the only way that damning evidence could be accumulated, to bring the organizers to justice, would be to breach the security of the country complex, situated in West Virginia.

I could have given evidence as to what had happened to me but I really needed corroborative evidence. In any event, I was certain that whatever was happening at the country complex also needed to be revealed to the authorities.

The FBI had no pretext and no basis for investigating the West Virginia complex, as it was apparently authorized to operate under the auspices of the Federal Bureau of Prisons. So I concluded that I alone had to infiltrate the complex secretively and accumulate sufficient evidence for the FBI to bring the perpetrators to account.

I had a meeting with the FBI and explained that, based on what I had been told by Antonio and his family and also on what I had seen, there was a strong likelihood of several criminal activities— drug trafficking; illegal drug manufacture (including illegal and unauthorized cultivation of marijuana); illegal transportation of aliens into the US; and crimes against humanity including sex trafficking, rape, kidnap, unlawful imprisonment and forced labor (slavery).

I explained that I had a plan to catch the offenders red-handed and bring them to justice without any legal or other evidentiary loopholes. That plan required me to breach the security of the country complex alone, so that I could obtain the evidence before the organizers of the complex realized that they were under suspicion. If they knew that they were going to be investigated by the FBI, they would no doubt have destroyed or transported any damning evidence to another location. Ultimately, they could have destroyed the entire complex by fire or some other contrived accident.

Once I had infiltrated the complex and obtained the irrefutable evidence, it was agreed that I would contact the FBI immediately with all necessary information for them to enter the complex, lay charges and arrest any or all for questioning and detainment.

An additional request was made by Antonio—he wanted to be present when the FBI made the bust, so that he could identify the men who had raped his daughter and those who had been complicit in turning his son into a heroin addict. The FBI acquiesced to this request.

Chapter 25
Preparation for Battle

By this point in time, Apollo Rhodes had evolved into a magnificently well-muscled and highly conditioned fighting machine, endowed with all the experience and training of his life as an ancient Spartan warrior and a World War Two US Marine Sgt. However, he would now need more than strength, physical agility and courage. He would also need to use all of the stealth, cunning and tactical skills that he had acquired over many years of training as a campaign veteran and leader in both ancient and modern warfare. He could now also use to advantage his newly resurrected and refined skills of extra sensory perception, mental telepathy, hypnosis and other mind skills that he had acquired and cultivated in his 18th century European life as a medical doctor and psychologist.

Apollo needed to prepare himself for the battle ahead. Unlike many of his contemporaries and peers from the past, Apollo had always viewed human life with the utmost respect. Even as a highly trained fighting machine in ancient Sparta (where killing one's enemy was considered a necessary, honorable, laudable and even desirable act), Apollo always respected human life and only ever killed in battle or when necessary to preserve his life or the lives of his people and loved ones. With disgust, he remembered clearly some Spartan warriors who would kill the innocent, the defenseless and the weak on the pretext that it was for the glory of Sparta.

Although there was no doubt that Paris Apollo was a patriotic Spartan with a deep and abiding love for his Lacedaemonian homeland (Laconia being another name for Sparta), in those times he often felt out of step with the zeitgeist of Sparta in 5th century BC. He often became angry at the way in which Spartan officials treated their own people, both young and old. He also deplored the treatment of the Helots, who were the subjugated non-Spartan inhabitants held in a state of serfdom. He would often whisper in a state of disgust, 'I feel out of place here. This is not my final home.'

Apollo's respect for human life was even more evident during his time as a US Marine. He always instilled the following ethos in his men:

*When confronted with a situation of kill or be killed, never hesitate for one second, because that one second could be your last. And when you need to kill, do so efficiently and without any doubt, because if your enemy has any life left in him, he may just kill you before he dies. By the same token, never kill for the sake of killing, when the life of the enemy could be preserved without risking yours or your fellow Marines. But you and your buddies always come first. So, if there is the slightest doubt, you **must** kill the enemy.*

In preparation for physical confrontation, Apollo needed his twelve to eighteen-inch sword, which the Greeks called a *xiphos*. This was an efficient killing instrument in close quarter combat. When he was fighting in the Persian Wars, he had to kill opponents as a matter of necessity, because the freedom of his kinfolk and that of Sparta and Greece were at stake. However, when in training or in combat with neighboring Greek city states, Apollo would often try to avoid killing his opponents.

If he could not overcome his enemy with blunt blows, Apollo would render his opponent helpless, by stabbing him in strategic points of the body. He would stab the back of the knee or thigh, in order to cut the hamstring muscles or tendons. Sometimes he would stab the anterior (front of) knee, rendering the knee useless and his opponent disabled.

Another Apollo ploy was to feign weakness or loss of balance by falling to the ground, whereupon he would cripple his opponent by cutting an Achilles tendon clean through. By targeting the lower limbs, Apollo was less likely to kill his opponent, but he would certainly render him unable to walk, at least temporarily.

If the opportunity arose in the course of hand-to-hand combat, Apollo would sometimes sever, with surgical precision, tendons in the anterior elbows or the shoulders of his opponents, to render them incapable of using their arms with any degree of harmful force. Apollo was always careful to avoid excessive blood loss; he had fought many battles and seen men bleed to death from severed arteries. He knew instinctively, and through harsh, hands-on experience, where and at what depth the blood vessels were located.

Such was the legacy of Apollo's beneficence and value for human life that, on any given day in Greece of the 5th century BC, where old, battle-scarred soldiers congregated, one might see a familiar sight—withered arms and legs belonging to disabled war veterans who were yet still alive. In those days, there were no orthopedic surgeons nor surgical hospitals where such injuries could be treated. It was left to the human body to repair itself as far as possible.

As a fighting hoplite or infantryman in battles between large armies, Apollo primarily used his javelin, shield and swords. Although he did not use a bow and arrow in battle, Apollo was an extremely accurate archer, having taken an interest in the bow and arrow from the time that he could walk. His family had worshipped the god Apollo as their patron deity for many generations. Apollo was the god of archery and his twin sister Artemis was the goddess of hunting. As 'the huntress', Artemis was renowned for her ability with the bow and arrow.

Although bows and arrows were not traditional weapons of Spartan warfare in the 5th century BC, Apollo, for the reasons stated, would use the bow and arrow if the enemy were at a distance. His reputation with the bow was legendary and he was often called upon when sharpshooting was of paramount importance.

Paris Apollo had won archery contests all over Greece. He would rely on his bow for hunting birds and small animals, but only in quest of food. He did not condone hunting as a sport, believing that it was not sporting to hunt defenseless creatures. As a worshipper of the god Apollo, he acknowledged that life, in all of its varied forms (human, animal and even plant life) was sacred and to be cherished and valued.

During World War Two, Apollo (then known as Peter Power) was very proficient in the use of a seven-inch Ka-Bar combat knife. The name of the knife was derived from an unsolicited testimonial by a fur trapper in the 1920s. He claimed to have killed a wounded bear with the knife when his rifle jammed.

As Peter Power, he was a master of hand-to-hand combat and he taught his recruits how to use the Ka-Bar combat knife. Consistent with his earlier life as a Spartan warrior, Peter Power preferred to wound and disable, rather than kill if the situation did not demand it. However, if his life or the lives of his men were even remotely in jeopardy, there was no more efficient killing machine.

The mission at hand demanded the silence and stealth of a stalking leopard. In his Spartan days, one of Apollo's solo missions had been to infiltrate the camp of an enemy army and return home with a specific item, as proof of his deed.

Even as a young teenager, Apollo had been trained in the art of cunning and catlike stealth by being required to steal food without being caught. If he had been discovered in *flagrante delicto* (caught in the act), he would have been punished with a severe flogging.

Apollo Rhodes' current objectives were to infiltrate the securely guarded complex without raising the alarm and then to accumulate an irrefutable body of evidence with which to convict those responsible for heinous crimes against humanity. The plan was to carry out this mission under the blanket of night. By doing so, there would be far less chance of him being detected. Only a select few FBI agents were aware of the clandestine mission.

The night had arrived. Apollo had to evaluate the situation directly, before deciding whether to go ahead with the mission. Despite the lateness of the hour (1am), it was a well-lit night, owing to a full moon and a cloudless sky.

Apollo was armed with a Ka-Bar knife and a short sword, which was the equivalent of his ancient xiphos. He also carried a collection of arrows and a bow similar to those used by peerless archers in Sparta. He wore a bulletproof vest to protect his heart and lungs, as well as a holster carrying a lightweight handgun, to be used only as a last resort. He was dressed completely in black, with black face paint to conceal his presence further.

Before emerging from the forest foliage, Apollo suddenly fell to the ground with great agility and lay prostrate to avoid detection. Lifting his head slightly and raising his eyes, he observed two burly armed guards on the perimeter of the installation. They were dressed in prison officer uniforms and were carrying high-powered rifles.

These guards were purporting to guard prisoners but, in fact, their primary purpose was to prevent outsiders from penetrating the security of the complex, thereby discovering what was really going on behind those prison walls. It is likely that when being employed for the job, these guards would have been told as little as possible, so that there would be less danger of them divulging any incriminating information.

It would later come to light that there was a hierarchy within the whole complex, whereby specialized workers within the installation would carry high security clearance while others, such as prison officers, would know very little about the internal goings-on.

Apollo knew from experience that it could prove to be a fatal mistake to underestimate one's enemy. Therefore, although relatively confident about having to deal with two armed guards, he balked momentarily when he spotted a third guard, who was even taller and more muscular than the other two. Given his gradually burgeoning strength and unusually rapid powers of wound healing, combined with his vast experience of hand-to-hand combat, Apollo was not afraid of these men. What he did fear was these men becoming aware of his presence and alerting the rest of the security personnel, thereby jeopardizing the purpose of his mission.

TOUCHING MINDS—ANIMAL MAGNETISM

Just as he had recently rediscovered (from his 18th century European experience) his powers of animal magnetism, whereby he could communicate with and influence the behavior of animals, so too was Apollo developing the ability to tap in to the mind of individuals, providing he had sufficient time to do so. Once he had formed a connection with a particular individual, Apollo could then communicate directly and subliminally with that person's subconscious mind. It was just as if he were communicating verbally with the conscious mind.

The tremendous advantage of a subliminal, subconscious connection is that the subconscious mind is far more receptive to suggestions. Subliminal suggestions do not run the gauntlet of the analytical scrutiny of the conscious mind, which can efficiently and quickly rebuff suggestions contrary to that person's will or belief system.

It is also important to realize that most animals, within the same species, act and behave according to instinct and that individual thinking is not a particularly dominant factor. Much more time is required to make a connection with individual human beings before the process of subliminal suggestion can be implemented successfully.

While in the process of transmitting subliminal suggestions, Apollo found that he could also access or tap into the current dominant thoughts of some individuals (in a sense, mind reading). This new ability was obviously incipient. To what level and how rapidly it would develop ... only time would tell.

The brick walls surrounding the prison complex were about twelve feet high and on top of the walls was a further four feet of barbed wire. There was certainly no way of climbing over those walls without risking severe physical injury.

The three guards were patrolling the full perimeter of the complex. They would occasionally stop to communicate on their cell phones. From where he was positioned, Apollo could only see one guard at a time. Occasionally, they would cross paths and gesture to each other.

In the area around the perimeter, there were several areas of discrete cultivation. Some were merely covered by netting erected in a tent-like fashion, while other areas were enclosed within glasshouses. They stretched for hundreds of yards. Most of the glass was frosted and the netting was several layers thick. Even from a low-flying surveillance helicopter, what was being cultivated could not have been determined.

The USFS (US Forest Service) in conjunction with the US Department of Agriculture often sent helicopters on reconnaissance missions, to search out the illegal cultivation of marijuana in areas of suspicion. The forested land surrounding this Federal Bureau of Prisons facility would normally be such an area of interest. However, the whole complex was classified on their maps as 'governmental' under the auspices of the Federal Bureau of Prisons, so both the complex and its surrounding precincts were not subject to normal scrutiny.

As he continued his surveillance, Apollo observed that the guards would occasionally patrol around the glasshouses as part of their watch. At one point a large truck appeared from a dirt road and was driven to the main entrance, where the driver offered one of the guards some papers. These were scrutinized by the guard, who then waved the driver through.

Apollo had been observing the three guards for almost an hour, focusing on their body language and gestures. He also began to home in on some of their thought patterns. He determined that two of them were reasonably benign and well-meaning souls, who were unaware of the nefarious agenda being perpetrated within and behind the walls of this institution masquerading as a prison. However, the one that Apollo spotted last was physically larger than the other two and gave Apollo a sense of unease.

From the telepathic vibrations emanating from the third guard's body, Apollo discerned that he had been involved in unsavory acts against innocent people in the past. It was entirely possible that he might have been aware of what was happening within the complex and that he was in collusion with the main offenders. Apollo had a strong feeling that the third guard had to be neutralized before he made his attempt to gain entry.

As it was nearly 2am, Apollo reasoned that the security measures might be relaxed slightly. He therefore attempted to telepathically place a suggestion in the minds of the two inoffensive guards that they should both take a break inside the walls and then promptly fall asleep for the following two to three hours.

Fortunately, that plan worked, leaving only one guard for Apollo to deal with. He knew that he had to disable the big fellow silently and quickly. This limited Apollo's options, as he had to ensure that the guard did not scream out in pain or for any other reason.

In addition to his weapons, Apollo had also brought some chloroform-soaked gauze; light but strong iron-impregnated rope for tying wrists or ankles together; as well as adhesive patches that would seal the mouth tightly and prevent any vocalization or screaming. Apollo also had a bag strapped to his waist, containing bolt and wire cutters and a state-of-the-art smart phone with in-built camera.

Apollo knew that he had to strike quickly if he were to have any hope of infiltrating the complex and gathering evidence before dawn. Accordingly, as soon as the guard turned his back, he silently and swiftly approached from the rear and delivered two firm karate chops to the carotid artery on one side of his neck, and the vagus nerve on the other. Those blows stunned the guard and caused disorientation long enough for Apollo to anesthetize him with the chloroform. Apollo then placed the adhesive gag over his mouth, tied his ankles and wrists together with the rope and dragged him into the bushes so that, when he regained consciousness, he would not be easily found.

Assuming that there were no guards in the vicinity of the glasshouses and the other plants being cultivated, Apollo determined to obtain some photographic evidence. After cutting through the lock to one of the glasshouses, he found what he had expected—cannabis. One of the plots being cultivated was covered with opaque plastic. Apollo easily cut through the thick plastic with his sword to reveal masses of cannabis plants which he also photographed. As he was doing so, he sensed the presence of someone looking at him.

Apollo turned around to find a stocky, pot-bellied, middle-aged man dressed in Prison Officer's uniform and pointing a rifle directly at him. Where had this guard come from? Apollo was surprised that the guard was so close, because he hadn't heard him approach. He had obviously been sent out from the walled fortress to replace the two who had gone in for their break.

As before, Apollo knew that he had to neutralize this guard before he had a chance to inform on him. The guard was standing about ten feet away and mumbled something about keeping still and not moving. He was about to reach for his communication device, undoubtedly to report to his superiors. Apollo knew that he must prevent this from happening. As the guard turned his eyes away for a fraction of a second Apollo determined to disarm him and prevent him from using his phone.

At that very moment, Apollo also perceived the presence of two distinct creatures. Within seconds, a snake, which had emerged from the cannabis plants where the guard was standing, envenomated the guard's lower calf with its two fangs, causing him to drop his mobile phone and rifle. Then, out of the blackness of the night and from the direction of the forest, before Apollo could completely subdue the guard, leapt a fully grown black cougar (or panther). It pounced on the guard with full force, rendering him semi-conscious. As the serpent slithered away into the forest, the black cougar stepped back from the prostrate man, indicating to Apollo that he could now take over.

Apollo recognized the snake by its markings and knew that the venom injected, although poisonous, would not be fatal. In addition to applying a tourniquet to his lower calf to minimize spread of the poison, Apollo securely tied up the guard, gagged him with adhesive tape and dragged him into the cover of the cannabis plants, to avoid early detection by his cohorts. Apollo facetiously suggested to the poor fellow (not really expecting him to hear) that he should avoid any unnecessary movement while he lay there overnight, as he might attract the further attention of the local serpents.

Having successfully dealt with yet another guard, this time with the help of his animal allies, Apollo swiftly finalized the accumulation of his photographic evidence. He took the liberty of borrowing the guard's communication device; he felt confident that he could imitate his slurred and mumbling tone, if called upon to respond. Apollo then emptied the rifle of its bullets and surreptitiously concealed it in nearby underbrush.

In the urgency and the drama of the moment, Apollo lost track of the big cat. After disposing of the rifle, he turned around to see the black cat looking at him intently with his golden yellow eyes. He returned the gaze and they connected telepathically. Apollo sensed that the cougar was telling him that, for the next few hours at least, he was at his disposal and that he could be counted on to assist Apollo's mission.

It was now 2:15 am and, as expected, there was only a skeleton staff within the complex. Apollo gained entry through the main gate by activating a specially concealed switch that he had seen the guards use. He had also relieved his unconscious 'friend' of his keys, which were necessary for full access.

CHAPTER 26
APOLLO GAINS ENTRY
TO THE COMPLEX

Apollo observed that, inside the high walls of the facility, there were several single story buildings. Two of them looked like army barrack dormitories—one for males and the other for females. They were both modest constructions, but appeared to be functional. Annexed to each dormitory were restrooms and washing facilities. Situated centrally to these structures was a long rectangular building, clearly used as a refectory or common dining room. It incorporated a large kitchen.

Standing out conspicuously from the basic buildings, because of its size and grandeur, was a two story official-looking edifice with a helicopter pad on the top. Its entrance looked like the facade of a hotel. However, instead of smiling valets or welcoming concierges, there were stony-faced armed guards, clad in their official uniforms. Two of them who were sitting in chairs in front of the building looked decidedly sleepy. This was hardly surprising, given the hour of the day. Luckily, due to their lack of vigilance, Apollo and his black feline friend were able to creep stealthily towards the building without being seen. Apollo telepathically communicated with the big cat, suggesting that it streak across in front of them as a distraction. This startled them and certainly aroused their curiosity.

'What in the hell was that?' quizzed one of the guards in astonishment, as he glimpsed a big black flash.

With his head down in the snooze position, the other guard murmured, 'I didn't see anything.'

The first guard continued, 'It looked like a huge black animal—a cat or dog—but it was moving so fast I couldn't make out what it was in this dim light. Maybe it was a black panther!'

'There ain't no big black cats in these parts; you'd have to go as far south as Florida before you'd find one of them black panthers in the wild. Must have been one of them oversized black house cats that's gone feral.'

'I don't know. It looked awfully big for a domestic cat.' The first guard shook his head in disbelief.

'Well, would you like to go look for it, then?' retorted the other.

'No. It's too dark. I think it'd be better to leave any search for feral animals until daylight, when we'll have a bit more backup.'

Just as he finished uttering those words, the black cat darted past again and surprised both of them. 'Hey, you're right, that was no house cat. He's a big sucker—a panther or a black cougar! Them animals are great climbers and it must have climbed the barbed wire fence in search of food. They don't usually come where humans live unless they're desperate for food,' remarked the previously disbelieving sentry.

As both guards became unnerved at the possibility of being stalked by a man-eating mountain lion, they lost their composure and were easily overpowered by Apollo, with the help of the black cat. They were bound and gagged and left in a dark secluded area of the facility.

It was now up to Apollo to gain access to the building directly through the front entrance, which consisted of a locked and heavy security door. Access through the front door was via an electronic card, which Apollo obtained from one of the guards without any opposition or objection. Prior to entering the building, Apollo donned the uniform of one of the guards, enabling him to walk through the entrance inconspicuously.

After inserting the card, Apollo slowly opened the door, peering through the narrow opening as he did so. There was an official-looking reception counter, but no-one in view. In keeping with the lateness of the hour, the room was only partially lit, but there was sufficient lighting to make out some detail.

It was also very quiet, with no sound of voices, so Apollo proceeded slowly, followed by the silent paws of the cat. When he reached the reception desk, he saw behind it another sentry, curled up in the fetal position on a black leather reclining armchair. To ensure that he did not wake up at an inopportune time, Apollo administered the chloroform-soaked gauze to his face and then bound and gagged him in the usual manner.

Apollo then ventured behind the front desk into an adjoining room, where he found the two guards who had been patrolling the perimeter. They were both fast asleep in stretcher beds, just as he had programmed them. Further out the back, he discovered a small dormitory for the security staff; beyond that was a kitchen and dining facilities. Fortunately, there were no other staff members to be seen.

Apollo returned to the foyer area to better understand the internal layout of the building. There he found a large elevator which had no buttons. Not far from the elevator was a door bearing the sign: *Private No Entry*. Apollo tried to open the door, but it was clearly inaccessible without a key. As he stood to the side of the door contemplating his next move, it suddenly opened. A tall, thin, tired-looking man aged in his late thirties walked through. Positioned behind him, Apollo took advantage of the situation and secured him in a hammer lock by using his superior strength. He then pulled out his knife and held it to the man's throat.

'Please keep still and quiet. I have no wish to harm you, but if you utter one sound without my consent, your life will be in jeopardy. As quietly as possible, I want you to answer my questions. Another incentive for you to do as you're told is the large black cat you see in front of you. He won't maul you, but if you don't cooperate, I can't be responsible for what the cat will do to you. Help me and you'll remain unharmed when I leave. Firstly, tell me ... where does this door lead to and where does the elevator go?'

The frightened man replied in a Southern drawl: 'Look mister, I've only worked here a few weeks and I've only done the night shift. They said that if I performed well then, after a few months, I might get a daytime shift. I've got a wife and a kid. I need this job desperately. I ain't had a job in two years, because of the downturn in the economy. I don't know much about this place yet. All they said was that it was a minimum security prison and, so long as I did what I was told, I'd do well.

'The only thing I know about the elevator is that from this floor it leads to the warden's quarters and then, above that, to a helicopter pad on the roof. I understand that the elevator goes down several floors from this level, but I don't know exactly how many. I don't have clearance to go down there. I'm thinkin' that something big is going on down there, but it ain't my job to know that. The lifts can only be used by the warden and a bunch of highfalutin security staff with special access cards.'

'Okay, you're doing well. Just keep answering my questions and everything will be all right. Now, where did you just come from through that door?' interrogated Apollo.

'I've got a key to that door. It leads to the floor above, where the warden has his residence. It don't lead anywhere else. If the warden calls me at night on my cell phone, I've got to go and help him in any way possible. He appears to suffer from insomnia and drinks a lot of alcohol at night. Sometimes he gets hungry and I have to bring up some food for him from the kitchen. I ain't got no access to his private living quarters.

'The warden has two security doors. I can't gain entry unless he opens the doors with his special card and keys. I've been told by my bosses that if there's any concern about the warden's wellbeing during the night, his living quarters may be accessed in an emergency by contacting a special number, but that ain't happened so far.'

'Did you just come from the warden's apartment when you walked through that door a few minutes ago, and was he awake when you left him?' enquired Apollo further.

The petrified prison officer answered co-operatively: 'Yes Mister. The warden was awake and he was starting on a snack and a drink. You ain't intending to harm him are you?'

Apollo answered the man sincerely, wanting to gain his confidence and maintain his continued cooperation: 'Look, my friend, I've no intention of harming anyone on this earth and that includes the warden and you. The purpose of my mission here is to help people by eventually freeing them from the bondage and suffering imposed on them by evil men, who need to be brought to justice.'

'You mean you're not a convict trying to escape? You're not trying to take revenge on the warden?' quizzed the perplexed officer.

'Of course not, my friend. I'm no more a convict than you are. I may as well tell you what this is all about. I consider myself a fairly good judge of character and, having now spoken to you, I know that I can trust you without reservation. The truth is that I'm working in cooperation with the FBI, in order to unmask a ring of—what you might call—big-time lawbreakers. They've perpetrated unspeakable harm and death not only on our fellow Americans, but also on innocent people throughout the world. Unfortunately, for you and for many other well-meaning conscientious employees of the US prison board, I have strong suspicions that this institution is being used illegally, for reasons other than the rehabilitation of minimum-security convicted felons.'

Apollo continued: 'But my suspicions are not enough. I must furnish tangible proof that will convict the offenders, beyond a reasonable doubt, in a court of law. You're in a position to help me in this quest; by so doing you'll go a long way towards absolving yourself of responsibility for being complicit with their crimes. Your job in this particular institution may be short lived, but if you cooperate now, I pledge that I'll do everything in my power to ensure that you're given another job by the United States government. That would safeguard your future, as well as the future of your wife and child, and any children to come. Do I have your support?'

'Sir ... as far-fetched as this all sounds, I kinda believe you. As I said before, ever since I started working here, I've had suspicions that something ain't quite kosher with this place. I think I'm goin' to have to trust you, and I will.'

'Well, let's get moving before the warden falls asleep,' said Apollo. 'It's imperative that I speak to the warden and that I gain access to those levels below ground. I need to find out in detail what's going on down there if we're to bring this heinous criminal enterprise to a close. I'll now resheath my knife and loosen my grip on you. But remember, my feline friend here is ready to pounce if you put a foot wrong, although I'm pretty sure you won't. By the way, what's your name?'

'My name is Lancelot ... but most people call me Lance,' replied the somewhat relieved hostage in a tremulous voice.

'Lancelot, let's get moving ASAP,' exhorted Apollo.

With alacrity, Lancelot placed the key in the door that led up to the warden's 'penthouse suite' as he said, 'Fortunately, before I came down, the warden requested me to bring a drink up to him. But, he sometimes forgets what he asked for or even that he asked for anything at all. I'll phone the warden before I ring his bell, so he's not startled … Sir, it's Lancelot. I'm bringin' you that glass of port you requested as a nightcap. I'm bringin' it up now.'

Apollo reassured Lancelot that he need not feel guilty about deception on his part, in allowing Apollo access to the warden's quarters. 'Lancelot, I'll pretend that I'm continuing to coerce you so that the warden won't feel betrayed by you. You must realize that this whole process is necessary if we're to expose whatever crimes have been committed behind the walls of this institution.'

CHAPTER 27
THE WARDEN

Apollo and Lancelot made their way up the stairs to a small foyer, where there were a few lounge chairs positioned outside the door to the warden's suite. As the warden unlocked his door, Apollo and the big cat remained to the side, outside the warden's field of vision. As Lancelot entered, carrying the warden's refreshments, Apollo and the black cat followed suit. Although he felt sure that he had gained Lancelot's confidence, Apollo pointed his handgun at the two men in order to ensure the cooperation of the warden and also to give him the impression that Lancelot was acting under duress.

The warden was a slightly built, balding man, aged in his mid to late-60s. Clad in sleep attire, he looked somewhat disheveled. He was thin to the point of looking almost gaunt. His wispy hair was silver in color. The smell of cigarette smoke was evident on entering the room and, as Apollo drew closer to the warden, the smell of nicotine was unmistakable. Not surprisingly, the warden was shocked by Apollo's intrusion and he became both agitated and tremulous when he spotted the cat. The warden was clearly unsettled by the presence of such a large feral carnivore.

After gesturing to Lancelot and the warden to sit down, Apollo directed his attention to the warden and addressed him with the firm voice of a man in control of the situation: 'I presume that you are the warden of this penal institution and that being the case, sir, I have a number of issues that I must discuss with you. Firstly, you must forgive your guard here for ushering me into your quarters. He simply had no choice, as you can imagine.' He waved the gun and pointed to the cat. 'Your guard put up valiant resistance to my insistence on visiting you, but to no avail. I just had to see you.'

As he listened to Apollo, the obviously apprehensive warden sat forward in his chair with his head down and his hands against his brow. He then raised his head suddenly and asked: 'Have you come here to kill me?'

'Sir, I did not come to this place with the intention of killing you or anyone else. I'm here with the express mission of seeing that justice is served, by exposing what I believe to be criminal activities inside the walls of this correction center. Look Warden, I'll get straight to the point. I've seen the marijuana plants being grown in abundance outside. The cultivation of those crops is blatantly illegal. Furthermore, based on information obtained from former residents of your institution, I have reason to believe that there's more than just marijuana cultivation going on here. My intuitive hunch is that, within the walls of this penitentiary, there is mass production of different types of drugs.'

The warden sat up straight in his chair and, with a pensive, wistful air of resignation, muttered softly: 'I knew this day would come.' He paused for a further moment of reflection and then, looking around the room for his bottle of gin (he had already consumed the port), asked politely: 'Do you mind if I pour myself a drink, Mister ... what is your name?'

'My name is not important at this time; you don't need to know it … just think of me as John Citizen, because my mission here is for the benefit of every John Doe and their families. All the decent people of this world and their children need to be saved from the bondage and the soul-destroying effects of illicit, addictive drugs,' replied Apollo.

After pouring his drink and imbibing half a glass in a single swallow, the warden commenced his candid narrative. 'Okay then, let me call you John, if I may. You know, John, when you came in here wielding that gun, my first impression was that you'd been sent by the big boss to knock me off.'

The warden paused for a few seconds, as though he was having difficulty getting his words out, but then continued: 'To be quite frank, if the big boss finds out that I've revealed the information that I'm about to divulge to you, my life won't be worth a red cent, but you know what? I'm beyond caring. My life is worthless anyway.

'I came into this job about seven years ago. The place had been here for about three years before I came on the scene. I was elevated into this position, following the untimely death of my predecessor in suspicious circumstances. I came from a nice, simple desk job in Washington's Department of Justice.

There seem to be two high ranking officials in the Justice Dept. who have the most say in the running of this place. One of them I've never met nor seen—he keeps a low profile and is very secretive. I don't know his name; so let's call him Mr. X. The other one—a thickset, overweight man— I've spoken to a number of times on the phone and have met briefly. His name is Damien Kadwinder.

'When I took this job, I was in desperate need of money. My wife had just passed away after a long illness, so there was nothing holding me in DC other than my three children. But they had all moved out of home and were busy starting their own families. I now have teenage grandchildren, but I hardly ever see them. Because of the remoteness of this place, they offered a higher than usual salary for a job of this kind. So, I thought I'd work here for about a year or two and then transfer to another job in DC or close by.

'Initially, when this facility was in the planning stages, it was known to be an area of West Virginia where illegal cultivation of marijuana took place. I think Kadwinder was part of a committee to select a site for, and then arrange construction of, a minimum security prison. My hunch is that he selected this site under the influence of Mr. X for less than honorable reasons.

'So Kadwinder selected this site with its already vast areas of marijuana cultivation. To make things look good, he issued an order to have the marijuana crops destroyed, before construction was due to start on the present facility. However, once control of the whole project was left in his hands, no other officials bothered to check.

'My impression is that Kadwinder, at the prompting of Mr. X, kept the cultivation of the marijuana going, on the pretext that it would give the inmates something to do. In any event, if questions were asked about it, his answer would be that the marijuana was going to be used for medical research into pain relief for terminally ill cancer patients.

'Honestly, I doubt whether any of the crops produced here have ever been used for medical research. My guess is that, through a select group of minions, who he's paid off handsomely, Mr. X has been able to establish a very lucrative business for himself in the drug trade. Yes ... I believe that Mr. X, whoever he may be, runs the show here! At the same time, I'd say that anyone who didn't conform just 'disappeared'.

'I also suspect that Mr. X has connections with Central American and South American cartels. Through the influence of these connections, I would guess that his cannabis business now constitutes but a small percentage of his drug trafficking empire. Those cartels have almost certainly introduced Mr. X to other more valuable street drugs such as crystal methamphetamine—better known as "ice"—as well as cocaine, ecstasy and heroin. Then you've got your hallucinogenic drugs like LSD and PCP, commonly called *Angel Dust*. There are other names that I can't even remember or pronounce, for that matter.

Look, John, a lot of what I'm telling you is guesswork and some of it may be off course, but I'm sure a lot of it is correct. Rumor has it that they're now working on a new drug down there that magnifies a man's physical strength and makes him impervious to pain. They're even saying that the drug makes him more obedient to orders—such a man could be programmed to become the perfect soldier. If this drug becomes available it could also be used by unscrupulous men in government, in sport or any other situation where physical prowess, endurance and stamina are the keys to success.'

Looking for reassurance that what he was being fed by the warden was true, Apollo probed further by asking: 'How do you know all this and why are you being so candid?'

The warden retorted: 'Look John, I've been stuck in this job for more years than a person should endure. I was hoodwinked initially into thinking that I'd landed a well-paid job that I could pull out of after a reasonable time of service. Unfortunately, I now know too much about the organization to leave this place alive! My phones and other communication devices are tapped at all times and they're regularly screened. Ironically, in some ways, I'm more of a prisoner here than the inmates.

'In order to ensure my compliance, Mr. X, speaking through Kadwinder, has made it clear that he knows where my children and their families live and that he's keeping watch over them ... in case they have any accidents. When you came in that door with your gun, I was certain that you'd been sent by Mr. X to assassinate me on the basis that I'd outlived my usefulness—in other words, I'd become more of a liability than an asset to his expanding organization.

'As I said to you before, if these guys find out that I've been speaking to an outsider ... I'm a dead man! I've been living my life with the sword of Damocles hanging over my head for too many years.'

'Damocles!' interrupted Apollo, attempting to interject a bit of humor into the warden's dour story. 'I once knew a Damocles; he was a fair swordsman at that. How did you come by his sword?'

'John, I'm referring to the ancient story, you know ... to explain that my life is hanging by a thread,' the warden replied glumly.

'I know you are, Warden. I was just trying to lighten the gloominess of your situation,' retorted Apollo with a mischievous but reassuring grin of optimism.

Overlooking Apollo's lightweight attempt at humor, the warden continued: 'Don't you realize that as soon as you notify your backup and the authorities descend upon this place, Mr. X and his acolytes will cast me as the informer. I'm not so much concerned about my own life but, if that happens, I fear for my children and their families. While Mr. X remains at large and free of any constraints from governments or law enforcement authorities, he wields enormous influence over so many lives through his many illegal connections.

'Mr. X has become massively wealthy and extremely influential in the USA and in many other countries throughout the world, through his numerous drug distribution outlets. He's become a power unto himself and is beyond the capacity of our legal system to control. The assets that he mostly relies on are his anonymity and his great capacity for fast transportability, which make him a ghost-like figure.'

'I see your point Warden,' Apollo reflected, with a contemplative look on his face. 'Yes, indeed, you're right. It's one thing to gather the evidence and to prove beyond doubt that crimes are being committed. It's another thing entirely to identify the perpetrator and then take him into custody. If we crash this facility, Mr. X will go into hiding, only to reappear somewhere else. If only we could identify Mr. X conclusively and then locate him without his knowledge.'

The warden replied: 'There are a number of high echelon scientists and administrators who work down there periodically ... my guess is that some of them would know the identity of Mr. X. On the occasions that Mr. X has visited this facility, he has arrived unannounced by helicopter and under the cover of night. I'm told that he's often in disguise in order to keep his identity unknown to as many people as possible.

'Despite my position of authority as the warden of this institution, Mr. X appears to have utter disregard for me. He inspects the three below-ground levels without any reference to me. Although I have access to those levels, I don't have access to specific high security areas within them.

'My job is basically to take care of and deal with the inmates in this institution. I've no control over who comes in or goes out of this place. That's a matter for others to determine. I think Kadwinder, as the representative of the BOP (Board of Prisons) for this complex, decides who comes and goes. But clearly, as the stooge of Mr. X, Kadwinder does his bidding. In fact, if you can find Kadwinder and persuade him to talk, you will learn the identity of Mr. X.

'John, I want you to know that I have no connection or involvement with the drug making industry within this institution. My knowledge of what's going on down there has come from what I've seen beyond the high security areas. Most of the information I've conveyed to you is based on my personal observations over the years or on scuttlebutt that I've overheard. I've also gleaned information from incidents involving inmates employed on the lower levels. One thing's for sure—between midnight and 5am, I wouldn't have a clue what's happening down there.'

In response to the warden's statement, Apollo came up with the following strategy: 'Warden, so far, only you and our friend Lancelot know for sure that this facility is under suspicion, and I want to keep it that way. I could wait for the first shift to come on this morning and interrogate the men in charge, but I'm sure that would get back to Mr. X before I'd even left the compound. So, for the moment, we'll leave things as they are. But Warden, in the meantime I know that you'll make sure that all the inmates here remain safe and unharmed. I want you to behave as though I've never been here. I want to locate the whereabouts of the mastermind of this operation and then capture him before he can escape.

'As you say, it may be possible to find out the identity and location of Mr. X through Kadwinder. From your description of him, I think Kadwinder may be the man that I know as the 'big man' or 'Mr. Big'. However, I'm sure it will not be easy to obtain such information, without the use of a good deal of cunning.

'The same applies to you, Lancelot. As far as you're concerned, until further notice you know nothing of me being here. I know that I can rely on both of you. I have become a good judge of character in recent times and my gut instinct tells me that you're both honest and decent men at heart. Therefore, I'm going to leave now without even going down to the below-ground floors. In this way, we'll maintain complete secrecy concerning the investigation. By the way Warden, I had to temporarily neutralize a number of your guards in order to get in here. Five of them had to be bound and gagged. With each of them, I also planted the suggestion that they would have no memory of what had happened to them. You might want to rescue them when daylight comes.'

The warden chuckled, covering his mouth with his hand, as he nodded his head in acknowledgment of Apollo's advice.

'Just to let you know, Warden, my real name is not John … it's Apollo. I must say it's been an unexpected pleasure meeting you sir; you've been a great help in my mission. Goodbye and good fortune to you and your family.'

Without any further discussion, Apollo made his way downstairs with Lancelot. As a parting gesture of goodwill and gratitude for Lancelot's cooperation, Apollo gave him a firm handshake and a gentle slap on the back. As Apollo (clad in the borrowed guard's uniform) left the main building, the black cat followed him through the entrance. After a brief but intense gaze with his golden eyes, communicating a sense of solidarity, the panther bolted into the forest.

Apollo then communicated with his FBI contacts in order to abort the mission for the time being. He did, however, request that the prison be kept under 24-hour surveillance. Any trucks going in or out of the installation were to be monitored. Any helicopters landing or departing were to be filmed, with special focus on the occupants. However, none of the workers, at whatever level, should have any cause to suspect that they were under surveillance.

CHAPTER 28
THE BIG MAN TALKS

Mr. Big (aka the big man) felt relatively self-assured and at ease in his top floor city location, with his helicopter pad and his security arrangements. Following the incident involving the heroin overdose within the walls of his establishment, during which both an ambulance and the local police were called, Mr. Big felt that any doubt about the probity of his organization had been quashed. The fact that he had a couple of local policemen on his payroll gave him further reassurance that the federal police would be kept out of the picture. But the answers that he had given to the local police, although potentially feasible, would not have convinced genuinely probing law enforcement officers.

Apollo knew the big man to be his would-be killer. However, that fact would be difficult to prove, given the manner he had come by this knowledge. Mr. Big knew Apollo as the young boxer who somehow managed to pull off a preposterous victory, after being knocked down for a nine count by a former contender for the world light-heavyweight boxing title.

Mr. Big also remembered Apollo as the frightened young man who happened to be in the wrong place at the wrong time, when he attracted the attention of Mr.Big's cohort of drug-dependent teenagers. In fact, the big man believed Apollo to be deceased, because he had sent two henchmen to eliminate Apollo as a potential risk to the security of his organization. The two assassins had injected Apollo with a lethal drug and had dumped him in the forest with only a covering of leaves as camouflage— destined to be carrion for scavenging carnivores.

It is not surprising that Apollo looked forward, with a sense of impish glee, to the sight of the Mr. Big's facial expression, when he came to the realization that he was not dead, as reported by his henchmen. It was with an even greater sense of satisfaction that Apollo anticipated the reaction of the big man's two bodyguards, when they were confronted with the knowledge that they had failed to kill him, despite their sophisticated and protracted efforts.

As there had not been any comprehensive investigation into the goings-on at the city complex, Mr. Big had decided to remain silent about the potential threat to their illegal enterprise. He wanted to escape any unnecessary scrutiny that would cause him to lose favor and trust with those to whom he was accountable. In the hierarchy of the criminal organization, Mr. Big ranked highly, but he knew it was prudent to avoid drawing attention to himself under the circumstances.

With the city complex essentially abandoned, the big man and his two henchmen, the Doc and Ape, were lulled into a state of slothful lethargy. Apollo decided to take advantage of their state of unreadiness, while stealthily breaking into the Academy.

Before they were aware of his presence, Apollo confronted Ape and Doc, both in a state of slovenly repose. Miffed at the treatment that they had previously dealt out to him, Apollo decided that it was payback time. After relieving them of their firepower, Apollo decided to give each of them a personal lesson in unarmed combat.

'You once escaped death by some miracle, but you won't escape us again,' was the Doc's feeble threat, as the pair were confronted by the challenging figure of Apollo. But despite their braggadocio, Apollo easily overpowered both of his opponents utilizing his vastly improved combative skills and burgeoning strength. They were soon dazed, bewildered, wincing in pain and unable to stand.

Unaware of the threat, Mr. Big bumbled his way into the area and, before he could raise his gun, Apollo administered a firm karate-chop to the big man's wrist, knocking the pistol out of his hand. Disarmed and in poor physical condition, the obese big man posed no threat to the magnificently muscled warrior. When Mr. Big saw with dismay that his two bodyguards had been bound, gagged and anesthetized by Apollo, he realized that any resistance was futile.

Stunned by what had just taken place, the big man did not recognize Apollo at first. But as he directed his gaze at Apollo, who was brandishing Mr.Big's pistol, the big man's brow furrowed in astonishment.

'Yes, look at me Mr. Big; look at me closely. Do you know who I am, Mr. Big?' challenged Apollo scornfully.

The big man hesitated and then stumbled over his words. 'You're that ... no, you can't be! No, I don't know who you are,' he said, pretending not to recognize him.

'Yes, I'm the guy that your pack of hoods rendered unconscious. Yes, and I'm the guy that you were about to shoot in the head, had it not been for the sound of police sirens. Yes, Mr. Big, I'm the one you ordered your two assassins here to kill, leaving no trace of the crime,' Apollo taunted.

'How could you possibly know all this? You were unconscious. You didn't see me. You're just guessing. You can't prove any of this,' retorted the big man defiantly. 'And stop calling me Mr. Big ... my name is Damien Kadwinder'.

'Kadwinder? ... Look, Mr. Kadwinder ... perhaps I can call you Damien, if you don't mind. We need to have a long talk. Your loyal, tenacious and vigilant bodyguards are still asleep,' commented Apollo sarcastically. 'But even when they wake up, they'll still be bound and unable to do anything. So why don't we just leave them here and go upstairs to the privacy of your office? There we can have a little discussion, where I'll ask all the questions and you'll provide all the answers.'

As they walked up the stairs, Apollo continued to implant suggestions in Damien Kadwinder's subconscious mind about being candid, truthful and informative in their dialogue. Apollo's hypnotic suggestions also emphasized the need for Damien to be comprehensive and to not hold anything back. Apollo suggested that Damien would feel so much better about himself, but only if he told the unadulterated truth. Apollo gave him a post-hypnotic cue that all of these suggestions would become even more imperative when Apollo mentioned the name 'Mr. X'. So, on hearing the name 'Mr. X', Damien would have an irresistible urge to discuss everything he knew about Mr. X, from the most minor detail to the most important information about him.

As he was passively ushered into Damien Kadwinder's spacious penthouse office, Apollo was impressed by the opulence of the decor. At the same time, he wondered how much illegally obtained money had been spent on furnishing such a magnificently appointed office. In the manner of a psychiatrist obtaining a history from his patient, Apollo gestured to Damien to recline on a comfortable-looking leather couch, while he occupied the overtly expensive leather desk chair.

Apollo commenced his interrogation of Mr. Kadwinder: 'Damien ... as big and important as you are in your criminal organization, I believe there's one other man that you must answer to—he is the mastermind and the evil genius behind it all. You might say he's your boss; without his leadership you would just be a small-time gangster. I don't know his name and I don't know much about him. Let's just call him Mr. X—please tell me everything you can about Mr. X.'

Under the influence of hypnosis and at the direction of Apollo, Damien commenced his long and detailed exposé. 'The man that you call Mr. X is actually ... Kurt Otto Von Grimmelhoff. He was born in the United States; but, from childhood, Kurt frequently travelled with his family to Germany—the birthplace of his parents. He's a tall, fit-looking man in his mid-40s, but looks younger. The families of both of his parents were highly favored in Hitler's Germany, because of their wealth and their perceived loyalty to the Fuhrer.

'Anticipating the inevitable fall of Hitler's regime, both families sold off assets and deposited the proceeds into Swiss bank accounts, using influence and connections established over several generations. Although they were prepared to accept the consequences of a German victory, they believed that to be unlikely, following the Battle of Britain in 1940 and Hitler's failure on the Russian front.

'After the Allies landed in Normandy on D-day (6 June 1944) and France was liberated from Nazi rule, the two families decided to move from Germany. When Hitler was preoccupied with his futile attempt to halt the unstoppable march of the Allies towards Berlin, the two families departed from Germany. They had purchased properties in both Switzerland and Spain, in anticipation of their eventual relocation.

'Kurt's mother was a young infant and his father about five years older when their two families, being longstanding friends and business associates, moved in unison to their respective residences in neutral Switzerland at the end of 1944. Post World War Two, the families remained firm friends and prosperous business associates. They remained in Switzerland, but spent the cold northern European winters in the warmer climate of Majorca in sunny Spain.

'As Kurt's parents grew up, it became clear that they were well suited for each other. The wealth and influence of each family was further consolidated by the union of the two children, in a similar fashion to arranged marriages among European royalty. The young couple were married in the late-60s and, for business reasons, they moved to New York City where they lived in a palatial penthouse apartment, purchased for them by their doting parents. It was in New York City that Kurt was born in the early 1970s.

'Given the considerable combined wealth of his parents and grandparents, Kurt received a privileged upbringing with no expenses spared in any area of his education. He was sent to the finest, most prestigious schools and colleges, where he showed great aptitude, but he tended to be on the perfunctory or lazy side when it came to studies. He was tutored in the piano and music generally and developed a great appreciation for the German and Austrian composers.

'Kurt obtained training in various disciplines of self-defense, including judo, karate and taekwondo. He also participated in fencing in college and won many trophies at intervarsity competitions. He would have represented the United States at World Championships level, but for a fencing injury at the time.

'Having plenty of money, Kurt often indulged in expensive illicit drugs such as cocaine, crack cocaine and marijuana. Unfortunately, in the process of experimenting with these drugs, he developed a personality change and became paranoid and violent at times. Eventually, he realized the folly of his ways and, before his parents had become aware of his drug use, Kurt managed to stop using altogether. He may still use occasionally—I really don't know.

'During school and college vacations, Kurt visited his grandparents in Switzerland, Germany and Spain. In conversation with his parents and grandparents, he only spoke German, and so remained extremely fluent in his ancestral language. Unfortunately, one of the legacies of his recreational drug use was the emergence of obsessional thoughts and ideas. He became obsessed with everything relating to Hitler and World War Two. He even developed an irrational obsession with the so-called Spear of Destiny. Apparently, one of Hitler's super-stitious beliefs was that he would have the power to control the destiny of the world if he possessed the Spear. Kurt's deep interest in the Holy Lance, as it was also called, was fueled by stories told to him by his grandfathers.

THE SPEAR OF DESTINY

Referred to in the Gospel According to John, it is also called the Lance of Longinus, the Holy Lance or the Holy Spear. It is recorded that one of the soldiers pierced the side of Jesus Christ with a lance as he hung on the cross.

'Some of his associates maintain that Kurt evolved into an obnoxious and manipulative narcissist and bully. Others have described him as uncompassionate and insensitive to the feelings of others, being only concerned with self-gratification. He was reputed to have espoused delusions of grandeur and to have demonstrated racist tendencies. So it's not surprising that many have asserted that Kurt became indifferent to the basic human rights of others and thumbed his nose at the authorities and their laws and rules.'

Apollo interjected with a critical comment: 'In ancient times, a mortal who showed disrespect or irreverence towards the gods was deemed guilty of *hubris* and was thus destined to suffer grave retribution by Nemesis, the punisher of the hubristic.'

Damien Kadwinder continued his discourse: 'Capitalizing on the international influence of his forebears and on his degree in political science and international relations, Kurt secured a job in the diplomatic corps in Washington DC. Being multilingual and especially fluent in German, Kurt became influential in the diplomatic circles of DC. Ironically, using his charismatic powers, Kurt was later appointed to a post in the US Justice Department.

'When I first met Kurt, I was also working in Washington DC in the Department of Justice. After a few years, I became a high-ranking official in the Board of Prisons (BOP).

'It was about ten years ago that I was given the job of selecting the location and then organizing the construction of a low-security prison and rehabilitation center for minor criminals. My appointment was facilitated by the devious manipulation of fellow committee members by Kurt. At that time, Kurt had already established marijuana plantations in Spain and Morocco to provide income for his lavish lifestyle. His fortress-mansion, located in an isolated rural area in northern West Virginia, was in the early stages of construction.

'Kurt needed a lot of additional capital to finance his project. He had already determined in his own mind an appropriate location for the new penal institution and strongly recommended the area where it now stands. Kurt's recommendation was based on the area's seclusion and the fact that marijuana had already been successfully cultivated there, without attracting the attention of the law.

'I don't know what it is about this guy. I guess he has some sort of sinister persuasive power over people ... he's a master manipulator. From the beginning, when I was asked to take on the job of selecting the site for the prison, I intended it to be totally legitimate. However, I compromised my standards, my principles and my morals and now this is where you find me. The facility that we're sitting in now was always meant to be a halfway house—the final destination for minor offenders or totally reformed convicts. It was meant to be a springboard to everyday life in our so-called 'law-abiding' society.

'Honestly, the primary purpose of the physical culture and development center, the healthy food restaurant and the nightclub was to assist reformed offenders to acclimatize to harmonious and healthy interaction in society.'

'Yes ... and like everything good in this world ... it had the potential to be corrupted from the inside out by the cancer of evil men's deeds or good men's inaction or acquiescence,' interjected Apollo with a wisdom beyond his apparent years, but reflecting a sagacity gleaned over several lifetimes.

Damien Kadwinder continued his confession. 'You know, I've never exactly been a pillar of moral rectitude, but when I got involved with this guy, I really let myself go. I started using guns and, after you kill the first man, it's not so difficult anymore. You become desensitized to it. I never really wanted to kill anybody. But when people get in your way or when they threaten you by meddling in things that don't concern them, then what choice do you have? It's either you or them. A man's gotta protect his interests and hold on to his life. It's a matter of kill or be killed.'

'How many times have I heard that one?' Apollo retorted under his breath.

But Damien was oblivious to the comment and continued: 'Anyway, construction on the country facility got started. Then Kurt decided that he wanted to build an underground complex of laboratories and rooms with Federal Bureau of Prisons' money. He said to me, "Damien, don't worry; I have a way of classifying excessive expenses so that they seem legitimate. No-one else in the Justice Dept. will ever suspect that the extra monies being poured into the construction have not been appropriately spent." I asked him, "What do you want with all these laboratories and medical rooms?" and he replied, "Don't you worry about it. Let me handle that side of the business." So I said, "Fine, I'll butt out. One less thing to worry about is okay by me."

'So over the next two years or so, all sorts of things happened. The construction was finished. Scientific guys from all over the place started coming in. Some of them, were flown in from overseas for short stints. Then I found out that Kurt had bribed someone in the BOP (Federal Bureau of Prisons) to overlook the fact that no-one was being sent to the city or the country facility from the maximum security prisons. In fact, Kurt arranged for illegal immigrants to be brought in surreptitiously. They filled up the city facility and then the country complex.

'Kurt kept telling me not to worry—that he'd take care of everything. I just had to pretend that I didn't know anything about who came and went from these installations. It was not my responsibility. As far as I knew, they were allocated to my institutions by the appropriate officials in the Justice Department and the BOP and I didn't need to ask any questions.

'I went to the country prison from time and time to sign off on things relating to the facilities below ground, but I was really just doing it on the instructions of Kurt. Our clueless warden there really knew nothing about what was going on in the underground facilities. He was only told that it was a US government-approved, top-secret installation and that he need not concern himself about it.

'Over the years, I've come to understand most of what goes on down there. But there is a lot of technical stuff that I still haven't got a clue about. All I know is this—they're producing a lot of expensive drugs down there which have made Kurt an amazing amount of money. And I've been getting excellent commissions.

'I've also heard recently about a super-drug they're experimenting with. That project involves using some of the inmates as guinea pigs. I understand it's ready to be launched on the world market and that Kurt has invited prospective buyers to his forest fortress for price negotiations.'

At this point, Damien started to falter and to look at Apollo as though he was coming out of his hypnotic state. Apollo therefore reaffirmed and bolstered his hypnotic state by again using the key words: *Mr. X.*

In order to keep Kadwinder talking in this hypnotic state, Apollo prompted: 'Damien, back to Mr. X ... tell me more about Mr. X, the man who you know as Kurt Otto von Grimmelhoff. I need to know the location of his forest mountain fortress. I need to know where Mr. X will be in the coming week. You'll do this for me, won't you Damien?'

Damien hesitated for a few moments then, with a glazed look on his face replied, 'Of course.'

Now, in his reinforced hypnotic state, Damien seemed even keener to cooperate with every question and request directed to him. It was as though Apollo had the power, through his hypnotic suggestions, to bring people to the point where they were not only prepared to give information, but were willing and eager to 'spill their guts', without holding anything back.

Damien continued: 'Look, I've flown there are number of times in my helicopter. The best way to access Kurt's Castle, which is the name we sometimes give to his hideaway— because it was modeled on a German castle—is by helicopter. Kurt has a helicopter pad, which can accommodate up to six helicopters at one time. I have a helicopter pilot who flies me there, so I couldn't personally direct you there. But I think I've got a map in one of my desk drawers, which I usually keep locked. Now, let me see ... where are the keys to those drawers?... Here they are!'

Damien then opened one of the drawers. 'Yeh. Here's the map. I don't really understand it, but there are some numbers here and letters which I think are coordinates. If you take down those coordinates, you'll probably find Kurt's Castle.'

Apollo continued his interrogation: 'Tell me Damien, what's it like at Kurt's Castle? For example, does he have a lot of guards? Can it be accessed without a helicopter?'

'It can be accessed from the surrounding forest area,' Damien replied. 'About two miles from the castle, there's an airstrip which Kurt constructed. This allows access for small to medium-sized aircraft. From the airstrip, there's a narrow road through dense forest also constructed by Kurt, leading to the foot of the castle. The castle has been built against the backdrop of an escarpment, which rises high above the forest below.

'At the top of the escarpment is the helicopter pad, which is surrounded by more forest. At the highest point of the castle—the helicopter pad—you'll find a flag carrying Kurt's family crest. If you examine the flag carefully, especially in one corner, you'll notice some archaic symbolism which you may find interesting. Kurt had that inserted himself.

'In order to reach the castle from the forest level below, there's a winding driveway built like a corkscrew, which accesses different parts or levels of the castle. There are multiple levels to the castle and on each floor there are several security guards. The castle is built against the escarpment and from the top, one can see for miles over the forest below. A large force of men attempting to storm the stronghold from below would be quickly detected. It would take a great deal of effort to break into this fortress, although it could possibly be done from the air using helicopters. But there again, Kurt has a very sophisticated radar system, which can home in on aircraft well in advance of their approach. So, if he chose to do so, Kurt could easily evacuate the castle, with his entourage, long before the arrival of any helicopters.

'He also has some anti-aircraft guns which can be deployed at very short notice. In addition, the helicopter landing area is usually camouflaged to such an extent that it's almost impossible to detect it from the air. It's made to blend in with the surrounding forest. In fact, the helicopter landing area can be rendered totally unusable with the flick of a switch and vice versa.

'Given the presence of all these facilities, I would say that unless somebody knew precisely what they were looking for, a plane or helicopter traveling overhead could easily overlook the existence of the castle. So, in reality, if you wanted to lay siege to the castle and apprehend its occupants with as little bloodshed and destruction as possible, it would have to be done from the forest below with a small force of well-trained commandos and probably under cover of darkness.'

Apollo interjected, mumbling under his breath: 'Alternately, it might be possible for one man to do it, provided he had phenomenal skills, together with stealth and cunning ... and a lot of help from unexpected sources.'

Damien continued his confession with a warning for Apollo: 'Even if your small force of men were able to ascend several levels from the forest floor, by overpowering dozens of security men stationed on each level, you would still be confronted by four further obstacles.'

CHAPTER 29
KURT AND HIS THREE WARRIORS OF EVIL

DIABLO

Damien continued his exposé: 'Your first obstacle would be on the third level from the top of Kurt's Castle. This level is guarded by the man who you luckily knocked out on the night of the exhibition boxing match. I'm sure he won't let you do that again. Notwithstanding your lucky punch, this man's still regarded throughout the world as a top-ranking light heavyweight boxer. People who know what he can do call him *Diablo* ... it means devil in Spanish; and he's aptly named. He's handy with a knife and even faster and more deadly with a gun. Diablo is a cold-blooded killer and he hasn't forgotten how you humiliated him on that night. He's out for revenge and, if he knows you're coming, you'd better watch out, and watch your back as well. First chance he gets he'll stab you in the back or shoot you in the back of your head. This guy has no sense of honor or sportsmanship and he'll have no compunction about bumping you off.'

THE ORIENTAL ASSASSIN

'If you're lucky enough to get past Diablo and reach the second floor from the top, you'll be confronted by the oriental assassin. No-one knows exactly where he was born or where he was raised; it was somewhere in Asia. Some say he grew up in a Japanese training camp for *Ninja* —others believe he was trained in mortal combat somewhere in China, Korea or Cambodia. All I know is that he's a master of the martial arts and unarmed combat and he can be very vicious. He's also been known to wield a mean samurai sword.

I once saw him cut a man's arm clean off with one blow from his samurai sword. Fortunately for the victim, a team of micro-surgeons was able to re-attach it. In fact, he's so good at whatever he does—they call him Kan-do. The most prudent thing you could do would be to avoid him. But if you can't, then good luck, you're gonna need it!' Damien advised sardonically.

GOLIATH

'On the penultimate floor are the living quarters of Kurt's most trusted bodyguard, the six foot nine inch, three hundred pound African giant, appropriately called Goliath. Where exactly in Africa he was born and raised is not known. It could've been as far north as Nigeria or Ghana or as far south as Mozambique ... or somewhere in between. It's hard to get any information out of him: he's laconic by nature and has become wary of people who ask questions. He was born about thirty-five years ago, but records weren't kept where he lived. The story goes that he was orphaned at an early age and he had to survive by stealing. As a young teenager, he got into serious trouble with the locals when he apparently hit an old man harder than he realized. The man died and Goliath had to get out of town in a hurry. He made his way to the coast and signed up as a cabin boy or stowed away, depending on which version you believe.

He ended up in Cuba, where he took up boxing in his late teens. He later killed a local boxing hero in the ring with a knockout punch, which caused his popularity to plummet. Forced to flee again, Goliath made his way to Florida with the help of his boxing manager, who promised to help him obtain American citizenship. He had reached the full extent of his physical stature by this time and was invariably taller and heavier than his opponents. Although phenomenally strong, he lacked coordination and agility and sometimes lost bouts on points.

Goliath was spotted by a wrestling talent scout who offered him a contract with a troupe of wrestlers in Florida. He was given the promotional name of The Great Goliath and wrestled under that name for two years. He caught the eye of one of Kurt's associates at a wrestling match and was asked if he would work as a bodyguard for much more money than he was making out of wrestling. He accepted and has since travelled with Kurt as his principal bodyguard.

Goliath's main asset is his enormous physical strength. If landed precisely and with full force, he has a punch which is potentially lethal. He seems to be impervious to pain and has a humorless, almost zombie-like demeanor. He's tight-lipped, rarely engaging even in short conversations. He can easily pick up an average-sized man by the neck with one hand and is capable of choking the life out of him. He's already killed at least two men unintentionally and who knows how many more he's killed with intent.'

KURT OTTO VON GRIMMELHOFF

'If you get past Goliath, then you have access to the very top level, where you'll be confronted by Kurt Otto Von Grimmelhoff himself. As I alluded to previously, Kurt is a very athletic man who's still at the peak of his physical fitness and agility. He's skilled in the martial arts but, above all, he's a world-class swordsman. He relishes nothing more than a duel with any of the several forms of swords, ranging from the foil and the epee to the rapier and even to the broadsword or longsword of the dark and middle ages. He especially enjoys a duel with a competent opponent. In fact, I've seen him engage in several duels, some of which have resulted in the unfortunate and, of course, accidental demise of Kurt's hapless opponents. Just so that no questions would be asked, the bodies were removed and disposed of without a trace. I think that some sort of crematorium was involved, but that's not my department. Anyway, I'm sure you get the picture—Kurt brandishes a deadly blade!'

Finally, knowing that Damien in his hypnotic trance was compelled to tell the truth, Apollo determined to extract a confession from him. 'Damien, isn't it true that you ordered your two henchman, known as the Doc and Ape, to murder Apollo Rhodes by injecting him with a lethal drug? And wasn't it your intention and expectation that he would eventually die, after being abandoned unconscious in the wilderness?'

'Yeh, that's correct. That Rhodes boy was becoming a nuisance—he had to be eliminated for the good of the organization,' confessed Damien without hesitation.

'And how many FBI agents have you murdered yourself over the years?' quizzed Apollo.

Sounding almost proud of the fact, Damien replied in a braggadocious tone: 'At least four, but probably several more. Some of them may not have been FBI, but I didn't have time to ask questions before I fired. There was too much at stake—that's the business we're in.'

With Damien's confession fully recorded and with similar incriminating evidence against the Doc and Ape, Apollo arranged for the FBI to place them under arrest, so that they could not communicate with Von Grimmelhoff or any of his cohorts. The information obtained from Damien allowed Apollo to locate the fortress where Kurt held court.

Chapter 30
The Assault on Kurt's Castle

And so it was that Apollo found himself in the forest just before the clearing that led to Kurt's Castle. He now knew with clarity the identities and the capabilities of the opponents he would have to defeat in order to bring an end to the evil reign of Mr.X—now revealed to be Kurt Otto von Grimmelhoff. The situation at hand exemplified the old adage: *To be forewarned is to be forearmed*.

Apollo knew that Kurt and his henchmen had to be defeated and rendered incapable of escaping. Only then could they be apprehended and prosecuted to the fullest extent of the law. However, before contending with Kurt and his cohorts, Apollo had to meet the challenge of nullifying the sizeable force of men patrolling and guarding the lower levels of the rustic fortress. From the information he had elicited from Damien, Apollo knew that among this force would be a number of men who had been treated with the experimental drug referenced by both the Warden and Damien in their statements.

This new experimental drug was the key to Kurt becoming a multi-billionaire and one of the most influential men in the world. It would also give him more power and influence in his perpetration of drug trafficking, human trafficking and other illegal money-making activities. In addition, he would have greater bargaining power with opposing international militant nations, willing to pay anything to gain a military advantage over their rivals. In fact, if he were to achieve his ultimate objectives, Kurt's power could extend beyond the reach of the FBI or even international law. That would be a disaster and an intolerable travesty of justice.

Apollo understood that the new drug in its injectable form was a combination of several drugs with a revolutionary new secret ingredient. The new drug had been developed and manufactured at the prison facility, using illegal migrants as guinea pigs. It was dubbed Ultimate X-Force (UXF). Recipients of the drug would have the stamina, superhuman strength and aggressiveness displayed by cocaine, crystal methamphetamine and speed users. At the same time, recipients would also experience the calmness, euphoria and analgesic (pain-free) effects produced by cannabis, heroin and opioids.

The new secret component, on which the entire success of the new drug hinged, gave UXF the power of sustainability in its depot injection form, allowing it to last up to three months before another injection was needed. In addition, the new ingredient imparted a convenient psychological effect upon recipients by making them more receptive and obedient to the commands and suggestions of those whom they saw as the most 'dominant influential force in their lives'. The latter would be those providing the injections. It was to them that the recipients habitually gave their cooperation, allegiance and obedience.

Some of the test subjects had successfully received the injections every three months for up to eighteen months. However, Kurt and his scientists did not want to disclose the fact that, before UXF lost its effect, (a medical phenomenon known as *tachyphylaxis*), there were quite a few recipients (as many as 50%) who could not last more than two injections before they died suddenly or became hopeless mental cases. These diabolically adverse outcomes were kept under wraps by Kurt and his team of scientists.

Even so, unscrupulous dictators and military leaders representing the countries or rebel forces (in civil war-ravaged countries) would not have been overly concerned with a quicker than usual turnover or loss of troops. Their only objective was gaining the military advantage that they were seeking. The use of cannon fodder has always been a commonly accepted practice among warmongers.

In the dense forest surrounding Kurt's Castle, Apollo paused in order to check the weapons and other paraphernalia that he carried with him. He was convinced that the best chance of success lay in the element of surprise. He would have relished the support of comrades in arms as he had done so many times in the past, both in ancient Greece and with the US Marines in the South Pacific. However, Apollo instinctively knew that he had to do this alone. But this time, although a lone warrior, he would have the help of higher forces.

Apollo realized that his mastery of animal magnetism and his ability to harness unseen supernatural forces in the universe were growing stronger. The memories of his 18th and 19th century existence as a medical doctor, psychologist, hypnotherapist, scientist and itinerant faith healer were becoming more and more vivid and real to him.

Apollo never ceased to be amazed by the dramatic and phenomenal life-changing effects that the lightning bolt had brought about in his present life. He also realized that the changes were not static. Apollo could sense subtle improvements in every aspect of his being. He felt more in touch with the universe and the higher Force for Good.

Apollo felt psychologically better every day and also physically stronger and healthier. He was aware of his ability to heal more rapidly. He wondered just how far this could go before it plateaued.

Apollo also contemplated the possibility of dying again. He had died before on several occasions. He knew what it was like and had no fear of death. He knew that once the spirit left the body, there was no pain. He also remembered clearly that his spiritual existence in the afterlife was a magnificent and heavenly experience. It was far superior to his earthly life, which restricted and confined him to a physical body with all of its frailties, weaknesses and vulnerabilities.

The innate drive to stay alive as a physical being is exceptionally strong and is perhaps the strongest of all human instincts. Apollo perceived that he had been placed on this earth again, as a physical being, for a specific purpose. He believed that the Force for Good that brings about physical conception in a mother's womb, intends for us to see out the full extent of our physical longevity, in order for us to disseminate goodness and love throughout the world.

Only when the physical body has fully exhausted itself, through the process of natural attrition, are we meant to return to our heavenly spiritual home. We're not meant to limit our physical existence by doing away with ourselves deliberately, nor are we meant to tempt fate by placing ourselves in unnecessary situations of physical danger.

Apollo was about to place himself in a situation of extreme danger, but it was out of necessity. And it was for the noble purpose of overcoming the forces of evil through the powerful Force for Good. Although Apollo would be the sole human figure involved in the assault on the fortress, once he had reached his objective, he would have the backup of the FBI and the United States government. Of even greater significance to the execution of his one-man campaign, Apollo would have the support of higher forces and mystical powers that few people could understand or even imagine.

Chapter 31
Only the Humble Man Will Be Exalted

In order to reach the top of the castle, Apollo needed to harness the forces of nature, especially the animal kingdom. With this in mind, as the shadows lengthened and the last rays of the setting sun were gradually disappearing into the blanket of night, Apollo knelt down on the forest floor to meditate and pray for a successful outcome to his praise-worthy mission.

Apollo knew how greatly the gods of Olympus in ancient times honored and rewarded the humility of mortal men. He was now impressed, by his sixth sense, with the overwhelming conviction that the Force for Good required similar humble recognition. Such humility and acknowledgement of the higher and greater power had to be demonstrated by reverent prostration, invocation and prayer.

At this magical twilight time of the day, Apollo communed so closely with the universal Force for Good that, for a moment in time, he believed he and the Force had merged into a single unit of immeasurable power and love. This galvanized his belief in the viability and the ultimate success of his mission. It filled him with a passion and determination to boldly and fearlessly proceed with the execution of his plan.

Apollo reflected on his ancient Spartan life, at which time he would have called upon the dedicated support of his namesake and patron god, Apollo, as well as Ares, the god of war. He would also have pondered whether the winged enforcers of Zeus would descend from the lofty heights of Olympus to spur him on to victory over his enemies. The winged enforcers were four in number—Zelus, Nike, Bia and Kratos.

THE WINGED ENFORCERS OF ZEUS

Zeus was the king of the Greek gods. To assist him from his throne on Mt. Olympus, Zeus had four acolytes who were his winged enforcers. They were siblings—the children of Pallus and Styx—each with different powers. Zelus was the personification of zeal and dedication. Nike was the goddess of victory. Bia was the spirit of force, compulsion and might. Kratos was the spirit of ultimate authority, sovereign rule and power. The winged siblings were what we would understand as angel-like beings in today's world.

In his prayerful and contemplative state, Apollo exhorted the awesome forces of nature to support him in every step of his endeavor. He also tuned into the magnetic vibrations of the animal kingdom, land-based and airborne. Even the mammals and fish of the oceans, seas and rivers (under the authority of Poseidon, god of the sea) were called upon to send forth their mystical and ethereal waves of communication in support of his mission.

At the completion of his meditation and prayer session, Apollo could hear the sounds of barking dogs emanating from the castle. He sensed immediately that the animals were expressing vocal acknowledgement of his magnetic presence. He guessed that they were German shepherd guard dogs, used by the security staff to assist them patrol the area. Apollo further discerned that the dogs would no longer do the bidding of Kurt's men, but would now offer full cooperation and support to whatever he might direct them to do.

Through his animal magnetism, Apollo communicated with the dogs and directed them to escape from the fortress en masse and head towards the woods. On the way, they were to enlist the aid of any other canine creatures (such as coy-wolves, pure wolves or feral dogs) that might be in the area.

As he looked on from the underbrush, Apollo counted ten German shepherd dogs bounding away from the property, followed by several security guards chasing after them. Thus, when the last rays of twilight disappeared, to be replaced by a cloud-covered canopy of nocturnal darkness, Apollo seized the opportunity created by the escaping dogs. He crawled his way stealthily into the grounds, avoiding the scrutiny of the obvious surveillance cameras set up on the property.

Kurt and his henchmen were on the upper levels of the castle, as predicted by Damien in his discourse to Apollo while under hypnosis. From their lofty positions in the castle, they could not hear what was happening at ground level. The penthouse area in particular was meant to be soundproofed, as that was where Kurt entertained and negotiated the sale of his drugs to wealthy foreign dealers and military heads of state.

Kurt could tune into the surveillance cameras which were on his floor and the floors below, but he generally chose to ignore them, as there had been no incidents throughout the time he had been living and working in the castle. On this occasion, he had given specific orders not to be disturbed, as he was attempting to negotiate a very important sale of his new drug UXF to a number of heads of state and wealthy businessmen.

Some of Kurt's scientific staff, who had been instrumental in the development of UXF, were also present on this night, to explain and demonstrate the drug to the prospective buyers. Over that weekend, the guests had also been entertained by a bevy of voluptuous young women who were part of Kurt's human trafficking trade. These hapless women had been kidnapped, drugged and coerced into prostitution, believing that submission was their only hope for survival.

The women who had been selected to entertain Kurt's clients on this particular weekend were an elite group, which Kurt referred to as his 'personal harem'. He had ensured their cooperation by granting them favors and special financial inducements, which were too good to pass up. Nevertheless, behind their seductive smiles and gleaming white teeth, without exception, they bore a deep-seated loathing and disgust for this man, who manipulated and controlled their lives. Perhaps this would be the night that would see an end to Kurt's malevolent influence over their lives!

Although some of the security guards remained behind to patrol the grounds, the majority had gone off to retrieve the dogs that had mysteriously bolted into the forest. Apollo overpowered one of the straggling guards, without attracting the attention of any of the others. He then donned the unconscious guard's uniform, in order to escape detection. So disguised, he walked as inconspicuously as possible into the grounds, as though he were returning from the chase.

While several of the remaining guards were engaged elsewhere on the property, Apollo sought out those men who he sensed were under the influence of the drug UXF. They were wearing different outfits from the guards, which made them easily distinguishable, but Apollo could telepathically perceive who they were by virtue of their overly exuberant and troubled brainwaves. As he approached a group of them, Apollo projected brainwaves of a positive nature, communicating the fact that they were now under the dominant influence of good vibrations personally represented by him. When he was within ten feet of them, Apollo verbally enjoined them to believe that they were now under the dominant influence of good. That being the case, they were convinced to follow his commands only, to the exclusion of all others.

This sad group of virtual automatons must surely have been approaching the end of their effectiveness as 'super soldiers'. Most of them appeared sickly, fatigued, pale and gaunt. They were totally unsuitable examples for Kurt to demonstrate the virtues of his wonder drug UXF to potential clients.

Even as Apollo approached closer to his objective, Kurt was demonstrating UXF to the prospective buyers, using victims who had only recently been started on the drug. Kurt was, of course, highlighting only the valuable qualities imparted by UXF that made them elite, indefatigable and invincible soldiers. Kurt and his scientists were emphasizing their fearlessness, aggressiveness, immense physical strength, imperviousness to pain, and—perhaps most importantly—their absolute loyalty and unquestioning obedience to the commands of their superior officers.

The group of seven men, whose loyalty Apollo had just secured, were in desperate need of medical attention. Although still relatively strong and capable of fighting, it was apparent to Apollo that, rather than more UXF, they urgently needed medication to reverse the effects of that drug.

As Apollo contemplated the urgency of his mission, the sounds of canine howls and barking, as well as a cacophonous mixture of animal noises and human screams, became louder every few seconds. Still undetected, Apollo looked up to see the guards, who had ventured into the forest to retrieve their German shepherd dogs, being pursued by a diverse collection of animals, domesticated and feral—they consisted of coy-wolves, coyotes, feral cats, two wolves, a mountain lion, two large black bears and their own guard dogs. At the same time, the bewildered guards were being dive-bombed from above by an assortment of ravens and hawks.

The guards, who had remained on the property, attempted to shoot at the animals. But before they could discharge a single bullet, they were overpowered from behind by the overwhelming strength of the seven men who now followed Apollo. The guards being pursued by the collection of animals were herded into an enclosed part of the property and, together with their cohorts, were securely bound and gagged. There they remained helpless, under the watchful guard of the motley collection of animal life.

Fortunately, all the noise and commotion at ground level failed to attract the attention of Kurt and his henchmen on the upper levels, so intent and consumed were they in attempting to finalize the contractual arrangements for the sale of drugs, especially UXF. Faint animal noises and human cries were heard by Kurt's bodyguards, but they were dismissed as the usual nocturnal tumult of the forest.

Apollo's one-man assault on the castle was not anticipated. However, despite the successful neutralization of the guards at the lower levels, Apollo realized that his greatest challenge by far lay ahead of him. He still had the element of surprise in his favor and this had to be maintained, in order to prevent Kurt making a last-minute escape in his helicopter. Such an escape by Kurt alone, or with his three henchmen, would nullify the impact of Apollo's campaign in the long term. If he got away, Kurt would just relocate and rule his evil empire from a different fortress—and no-one could predict where that would be.

CHAPTER 32
THE NIGHT OF MORTAL COMBAT

As he entered the level third from the top, Apollo found Diablo, the South American boxer who he had knocked out in the exhibition match at the Academy of Self-Defense. Diablo was preoccupied with the company of two young ladies, undoubtedly from Kurt's collection of selected women. As Apollo approached the trio, Diablo turned around, alerted by the surprised look on the faces of his companions. Anticipating an imminent confrontation, the girls scattered, leaving the two men to face each other.

Caught by surprise, Diablo lunged desperately for the revolver in his gun-belt, which was hanging on the chair close by. As Diablo clutched the gun and aimed to fire it, Apollo, with lightning speed, drew two six-shooters from a figure-of-eight holster attached to his chest and blasted the gun out of Diablo's hand with both bullets hitting their mark. One of the bullets also grazed the flesh at the base of Diablo's right thumb, drawing blood.

With both guns trained on Diablo's chest, Apollo held the upper hand. But, in an act of defiance, Diablo challenged Apollo's spirit of sportsmanship (which was decidedly lacking in Diablo) by daring him to use just his fists, in an impromptu rematch of their bout at the Academy.

Apollo knew full well that he would be giving Diablo an opportunity which he did not deserve, but he was buoyed by supreme confidence in his ability to defeat his opponent in any form of physical contest. So Apollo magnanimously returned his guns to their holsters and raised his fists in preparation for a bare-knuckle fistfight.

With his strong Spanish accent, Diablo remarked quizzically, 'I thought you were dead. I heard that a couple of our boys had put you away for good'.

'As our great American novelist, Mark Twain, once said: "Rumors of my death have been greatly exaggerated",' retorted Apollo jocularly.

'Don't you know that I once fought the light heavyweight boxing world champ and should have had the victory on points, but for those crooked hometown judges? You were very lucky last time we met, *hombre*. But now I'll give you the beating you deserve,' taunted Diablo.

Provoked by Diablo's bravado, Apollo doffed his guns and shirt revealing a chiseled torso, with much more impressive muscle definition than had been evident when last they fought. Even Diablo, evidenced by his sudden crestfallen expression, was clearly surprised and intimidated by Apollo's bulging biceps and pectorals.

'You look strong and well built, young *gringo*, but can you box? Ha, ha... I don't think so,' scoffed Diablo.

Incited by those provocative taunts, Apollo decided to dispatch this annoying man without further ado. Utilizing his vastly improved reflexes and agility, Apollo easily evaded every attempt by Diablo to land a punch. In reply, Apollo dealt his opponent several bone-crunching blows to the rib cage and upper abdomen, which made the South American ex-boxing champ reel back from the devastating force of the impact.

Sensing that Apollo was more than a match for him, Diablo desperately grabbed for a large knife, which had been hidden beneath his coat. With the ferocity of a man fighting for survival, Diablo lunged at Apollo's heart. But Apollo easily disarmed him, at the same time snapping Diablo's right wrist.

Apollo looked down on his defeated opponent, who was buckling at the knees and knew that Diablo would neither comprehend nor remember what he was about to hear. Then, with a deep sense of pride, Apollo exclaimed: 'By the way, I was also a boxing champion—the heavyweight champion of the U.S. Marine Corps—before you were even born. We have an old saying in the Corps: *Once a Marine, always a Marine.*' And with that revelation, Apollo dealt him a knockout right cross, which left his opponent temporarily unconscious. He then handcuffed Diablo to one of the fixtures, rendering him totally ineffectual.

The two girls, who had fled to stay out of harm's way, cautiously emerged from their hiding place. They had witnessed the whole contest and were clearly pleased at the outcome.

'Hey Mister, where did you learn to shoot so fast?' asked the glamorously dressed young brunette.

'Wow, you look so strong; and what a punch!' declared the blond beauty by her side.

'Are you girls okay?' enquired Apollo. 'I can't answer any questions at the moment but, suffice it to say, I learned to shoot from a highly qualified man, but that was a long time ago. It'll have to be a story for another day. Anyway, your friend here is dazed for the moment, but will eventually recover to face the judgment of the court.'

'That beast is not our friend,' the brunette declared vehemently.

'We hate him with a passion!' added the blonde. 'This animal has raped us—both of us—so many times that we've lost count. Sure, we get regular medical check-ups and the best medication that money can buy, but only because we're young and attractive to men like this disgusting creep lying on the floor. I should spit in his face. This evil man has treated us as his sex slaves for the past year. We've been pampered with the best clothes, jewelry, accommodation and food—but only so long as we toed the line and did exactly as were told. Regrettably, we've been forced to sleep with the devil.

'Another young girl ... who was our friend, didn't do as she was told; she rebelled and now she's dead. They say she fell to her death by accident while trying to escape from this place, but clearly, Gina—that was her name—was murdered by this man and his evil buddies. She had no funeral and no burial. There's no grave site or headstone that we can visit to honor her memory. It's as though she never existed—except in our memories. In this mansion we're just like birds in a golden cage: we have everything except our freedom. Please, Mister, can you get us out of here?'

'Ladies, the very reason I'm here tonight is to bring an end to the evil empire of the tyrannical drug baron that Diablo works for. The success of my mission will also be what frees you tonight. But girls, you must help me!' exhorted Apollo. He then explained in more detail the reason for his mission and the need for it to be a one-man assault.

Now convinced that the best chance of extricating themselves from their wretched life of subjugation lay in the ultimate success of Apollo's mission, the two girls sprang zealously into action. Having been virtual prisoners in the complex for nearly two years, they knew all of the secret passageways and doors that would enable Apollo to access the next three levels above them without being detected. Apollo could not reach and apprehend Kurt until he had successfully overcome both Kan-do and the giant Goliath. Those two, as well as Diablo, had been strategically located in the castle as both a hedge of protection and an early warning for Kurt in the unlikely eventuality of the castle being besieged from the ground. That would then give Kurt ample time to escape by plane or helicopter.

Armed with this information and guided by the girls, Apollo was soon on the level occupied by Kan-do. As Apollo furtively entered the self-contained luxury apartment, he could see the oriental warrior through the door which was slightly ajar. Kan-do was seated Japanese-style at a banquet meal, which was being served to him by a bevy of oriental beauties.

The prospect of having to subdue Kan-do was a daunting one, but Apollo had observed him at the Academy of Self-Defense and had made a mental note of Kan-do's strengths and weaknesses. Apollo knew that his opponent would be very strong, as evidenced by his massive musculature and very broad shoulders. Kan-do was also stocky with well-muscled thighs and calves, which would make it very difficult to get him off his feet.

Being closer to the top level, Apollo needed to refrain from discharging firearms, for fear of being detected. So, he decided to adopt the direct approach. He just sauntered into the room where Kan-do was dining.

'How you get in here?' queried Kan-do in broken English with a distinctive oriental accent. Kan-do was both surprised and concerned at the sudden appearance of someone who he vaguely recognized. 'I see you before somewhere,' commented the puzzled Kan-do.

'Your door was slightly ajar, so I didn't think you'd mind if I let myself in, especially since Mr. Kurt said it was urgent. I started working for Mr. Kurt only recently. You may have seen me upstairs. In fact, Mr. Kurt has sent me to tell you to join him upstairs to discuss something.'

By claiming to be a member of staff, Apollo was hoping to lull Kan-do into a false sense of security, which would then more easily allow him to subdue the oriental powerhouse.

While pretending to process the explanation being offered by Apollo, the instinctively suspicious Kan-do calmly reached for a samurai sword mounted on the wall closest to him and drew it from its scabbard. He then turned around, gazing intently at Apollo with a threatening, sardonic grin on his face. With a stentorian roar that made his attendant females scatter in all directions, Kan-do exclaimed angrily: 'You lie! My door always lock. You break in my home. You not work for Mr. Kurt. I 'member you now. You knock out my friend Diablo. Them say you dead. You die now. I cut you head off!'

With those threats ringing in his ears, Apollo knew that the jig was up, but he had bought time and that was his only expectation. He knew Kan-do would not be so trusting as to accept his explanation.

As the ponderous Kan-do lunged at him with his samurai sword, Apollo was able to evade the lethal blade with his superior agility. Simultaneously, Apollo took advantage of his opponent's excessive weight and forward momentum by tripping him. With his ungainly body habitus, Kan-do lost his balance and fell prostrate, face down, hitting his head on the rock hard floor.

While momentarily dazed, Kan-do was vulnerable. Seizing the opportunity, Apollo, used his razor-sharp knife to sever the tendon at the back of one of Kan-do's knees, thereby rendering him crippled. Unable to get to his feet, Kan-do was disabled. After quickly handcuffing Kan-do to one of the fixtures in the room, Apollo applied a bandage to the wounded leg, in order to stem the flow of blood. And so it was that the fearsome and combative Kan-do was brought to his knees by the superior power of Apollo.

THE AFRICAN GIANT

Ascending to the penultimate level, Apollo realized that he could soon be facing his most formidable opponent ever— Goliath, the African giant. His reputation and immense size had filled many boxing and wrestling opponents with trepidation and fear.

Apollo always respected his opponents and evaluated their strengths and weaknesses very carefully as part of his combative strategy. However, he never feared them because it had been part of his training from his boyhood in Sparta. Fear was not part of Apollo's vocabulary, because he had been taught to endure pain and hardship without complaint.

The level occupied by Goliath was the most luxurious of all the apartments other than the top floor, which was Grimmelhoff's domain. To get to the top floor from below, one had to go through Goliath's apartment. There was also a buffer zone between the two top levels. It was essentially a storehouse for food items and beverages— an immense larder and pantry. The buffer zone could be bypassed by a 'special access' passage.

At any time, Goliath or his most trusted subordinates could be on any of the three top levels. Being the closest living area to Kurt's top level, Goliath's quarters had to be the most secure. Accordingly, there were closed circuit cameras monitoring all movements, unless the cameras were turned off by Goliath himself.

Apollo assumed that Goliath would be more inclined to deal with intruders using hand-to-hand combat, because of his size, strength and air of invincibility. Under such circumstances, Apollo considered that the best way to initiate an encounter with the giant would be by seeking direct entry through his front door.

Using the intercom, Apollo stated that he was there at the behest of Kurt and needed to hand a message to Goliath personally. The metal detectors did not reveal any metallic weapons, so Apollo was allowed to enter. As he was ushered into one of the side rooms by an attractive young female attendant, Apollo caught sight of the giant's massive physique being oiled and massaged by a buxom blonde female masseuse.

Goliath glanced at Apollo but did not recognize him, although they had seen each other before at the Academy. 'Boy—what message?' he enquired. Apollo handed him a note with the following words: *Surrender now to the Force for Good.*

Goliath slowly rose from the couch with a perplexed and ominous look on his face. Looking more intently into Apollo's face, the African behemoth demanded, in an angry tone: 'This was not written by Mr. Kurt. Who are you?'

'I am your nemesis,' declared Apollo.

Without fully understanding what Apollo meant, the giant nevertheless now knew that Apollo had gained entrance to his private domain under false pretenses. For that reason alone, he was incensed. Raising himself to his full height of six foot nine inches, the impressively chiseled muscles of the former boxer and wrestler gave him a distinct air of indestructibility.

The towering figure of Goliath would have intimidated most men, but Apollo had a plan. He knew that two essential strategies had to be implemented in order to defeat a man of Goliath's gargantuan size and immense strength. The first was to avoid close physical contact and so prevent him from taking full advantage of his superior mass and brawn. The second strategy was to get Goliath off his feet, so that he would no longer have the advantage of height and mobility. With the latter strategy in mind, Apollo had carried with him a weapon, called a bolas, with which he had become adept. This was a length of durable string or leather cord to which wooden balls were attached. When hurled at one's opponent with skilled precision, the string would wrap around his ankles, rendering him incapable of walking.

As Goliath attempted to grasp his opponent with his mighty arms, Apollo made a strategic retreat, to give himself enough distance to utilize the bolas. With great speed, Apollo whirled the weapon furiously above his head and then, with devastating accuracy, let it fly towards the giant's legs, below his knees.

The tottering titan lost his balance and crashed to the ground, face first. While Goliath was lying prostrate on the floor, Apollo securely tied his hands behind him with strong rope, before he could regain his equilibrium. He then cuffed his ankles together to render him immobile. Finally, to ensure that he could not break his bonds and escape, Apollo applied a soporific dose of chloroform to his face, allowing sufficient time for it to take effect.

Goliath's female attendants stared in amazement at the ease with which the giant was subdued. The women, who acted as housekeepers and servants, had no great affection or loyalty for Goliath. They had submitted to his demands and whims out of fear for their own wellbeing. They also feared retribution against their families, from whom they were often separated for long periods.

'Ladies, I request that you do not assist this man in any way that might enable him to escape,' exhorted Apollo. 'The federal police, the FBI, will come to arrest him in due course, in order to face charges.'

'You can be assured that we won't stand in the way of the justice system,' declared the masseuse, apparently speaking on behalf of the others. With that declaration, the three women departed without delay, realizing that they now had a window of opportunity to escape.

So, having neutralized Kurt's three elite bodyguards, it was now time for Apollo to confront the despicable mastermind behind this far-reaching international criminal organization. That evil genius had to be stopped!

CHAPTER 33
THE HAUGHTY SHALL BE LAID LOW

On the top floor of the castle was Apollo's main objective —the nefarious emperor of organized crime, Kurt Otto von Grimmelhoff. While Apollo was gradually making his way to the top, a collection of additional wildlife allies had gathered in the area of the helipad.

Following instructions from Apollo, three of the seven drug-abused men, who had allied themselves with Apollo, had proceeded to the very top of the fortress. There, with assistance from Apollo's animal friends, they had overcome the pilots and maintenance crew of both Kurt and the prospective buyers of drugs. So, there was no possibility for Kurt or any of his potential customers to escape.

Securely bound and confined to a small area on the roof of the castle, there was no way that aircraft of any kind would be leaving the fortress. A pack of wolf-like dogs were also there to thwart any attempts at escape by the beleaguered pilots.

As they stealthily descended from the roof to the living quarters occupied by Kurt, the three men were accompanied by a pair of wolves, a couple of cougars and a large black bear. The trio firmly, but diplomatically, directed the visiting drug clients and their entourages to confine themselves to their designated bedrooms, which were locked and guarded.

When Apollo entered the luxurious and elegantly appointed office occupied by Kurt, three security men halted his incursion by drawing their pistols, aiming them directly at Apollo's chest. Asked to identify himself or they would shoot, he nonchalantly replied, 'My name is of no importance but, if you must know, it's Rhodes, Apollo Rhodes.'

With a subtle German accent, acquired from many years of speaking German and European travel, Kurt Otto Von Grimmelhoff interjected: 'Mr. Rhodes, you are decidedly lacking in good manners. I don't remember meeting you or inviting you here. Nevertheless, are you interested in buying my drugs? ... Security! How did this man get on this level without my knowledge? Where are my three elite bodyguards?'

The head of security replied: 'We have just tried to contact all three, but there seems to be no answer.'

'Mr. Rhodes, if you are a member of the entourage of one of my clients, I suggest you identify who you're with immediately or else I'll have to command my security men to shoot you.'

Apollo continued to demonstrate an air of calmness in order to buy time, during which he expected the three security men to relax the intensity of their watchfulness. He replied to Kurt's question with a circuitous and disingenuous answer. As he did, Apollo noticed one of the security men drop the aim of his gun to the floor. Continuing to talk in a rambling fashion, Apollo seized the opportunity, and with lightning fast reflexes disarmed the security man by dislocating his elbow. Then, using the disabled man as a human shield, Apollo blew the guns out of the hands of the other two security men with pinpoint accuracy, before they had a chance to discharge their pistols.

Apollo ordered the men to tie up one another, using the strong rope he carried with him. Now securely bound and immobile, lying side by side on the floor, they no longer constituted a threat.

With the gun now trained on him, Kurt knew that he was cornered. But, Kurt—the wily fox that he was—decided to appeal to Apollo's sense of fairplay, which he instinctively sensed was integral to his character. 'Mr. Rhodes, you're obviously very skilled in the use of handguns and you've clearly gained the advantage with that deadly weapon pointed at me. But I wonder how skilled you are in the ancient art of swordsmanship?

'You've rudely entered my domain uninvited and threatened me and my staff with your gun, for reasons that are not entirely clear to me as yet. If you have any sense of decency and etiquette, I demand that you lay down your gun and accept my challenge to a duel, with any or all of the variety of swords which I have on hand.

' I perceive you to be a fair-minded man, Mr. Rhodes. So I'm sure you'll agree that any grievances you have against me personally or against my organization can be dealt with in the civilized, old-fashioned way.'

'I'm all for "the old-fashioned way"—been there, done that,' quipped Apollo, much to Kurt's puzzlement. 'As far as "civilized" is concerned—that depends on my opponent. I must admit... you're quite a persuasive and eloquent speaker, Mr.Von Grimmelhoff; but you're really not in a position to demand anything. Be that as it may, your appeal to my deep-seated sense of sportsmanship has certainly struck a chord with me.

'I'm definitely not one to decline a challenge, especially a duel, even where the stakes are very high and the outcome is crucial to many others over and above myself. As you would expect, I've done my research and I'm aware that you are a swordsman of Olympic standard. Nevertheless, as I've also done some sword fighting in the past, I'm going to accept your challenge.'

'Splendid! That's the spirit. I have a collection of swords in this cabinet. With your permission—seeing that you're holding a gun on me—I'll take them out of the cabinet.'

'Go right ahead. I'm curious to see your collection.'

APOLLO RHODES—MASTER SWORDSMAN

Not only had Apollo gained considerable experience as a swordsman in Sparta, he had also refined his skills in the art of fencing when a university student in Europe at the end of the 18th century. Apollo had been trained and mentored by some of the finest swordsman in Europe and had distinguished himself in many contests conducted in that era. The ability to be adept with the sword was vital at a time when brigands preyed on the defenseless, corruption was rife and the law was seldom enforced in a just and equitable manner.

Kurt then laid out on his desk three types of swords in pairs: a heavy type of broadsword from the Middle Ages; a rapier-like sword from the 16th century and a lighter type of foil, which Kurt preferred, from the 18th and early 19th centuries.

'Mr. Rhodes, in accordance with your agreement, would you kindly drop the gun so that we can proceed with the duel?'

Apollo did not drop the gun but replaced it in his holster.

'Now, Mr. Rhodes, you may choose the weapon with which to start our duel.'

Apollo pondered momentarily, then made his selection. 'Let's start with the sword which is the oldest of the three: the broadsword'.

Apollo had obtained experience with similar-sized swords in Sparta, but the sword with which he was most familiar from that era was the much shorter Spartan xithos. Nevertheless, he was extremely proficient with swords up to three feet in length. With his youth and superior strength, not to mention his past-life experience, Apollo definitely had the advantage with the heavy broadsword.

'Let the duel begin!' announced Kurt. 'Your sporting gesture to accept my challenge was a virtuous and commendable act, but a foolish and gullible one. It may even cost you your life. You see, Mr. Rhodes, not only have I been an Olympic competitor and would easily have won a fencing gold medal had I not been injured, I'm still one of the world's greatest exponents of fencing. You don't stand a chance against me. I find it pathetic that people like you allow their emotions to get in the way of rational, pragmatic decisions. That will lead to your inevitable downfall. The key to my success and my motto is: *Show no mercy and take no prisoners.*'

Spurred on by Kurt's insults, Apollo attacked fiercely with the heavy sword, surprising Kurt with the ferocity and the vigor of his offence. Kurt countered defensively and, with a sense of desperation in his voice, he again appealed to Apollo's sense of sportsmanship with a jocular remark, 'Take it easy, Mr. Rhodes. Are you trying to kill me?'

'I've no desire to kill you, Mr. Von Grimmelhoff, only to subdue you, so that you can be brought to justice and stand trial for your crimes,' retorted Apollo, in a more serious tone.

'So, I gather that you **are** a policeman, Mr. Rhodes?' quizzed Kurt. Apollo did not reply.

Kurt started to harangue Apollo: 'You mentioned the word 'crimes'. Who's to say who the criminal is in this situation? Could it not be you who is the criminal, for invading my domain and my privacy? Is it not up to the victor in any battle or war to decide what crimes have been committed and who has committed those crimes?

'History is always written by the victors, and the victors can sometimes be the criminals or, at least, be responsible for some blame in wartime by virtue of their actions or even their omissions. The first casualty of war is often the truth.

'Who's to say what constitutes a crime or an immoral or unethical act? The norms of society create the answers to those questions. Who's to say what's right and what's wrong, if not the existing culture? There are no absolutes, my young friend. There is no right or wrong. There is no good and there is no evil; it's all relative. It all depends on what society dictates and what society will accept.

'In my book, history will tell you that I have **not** committed any crimes. I have only appropriated what is rightfully mine. I'm entitled, as a superior human being, to seek after and obtain what is my birthright—spectacular success with its many facets.

'You might call me a go-getter. People who are lazy, ignorant or uneducated deserve to be led by their more educated and more knowledgeable superiors. The ancestors of superior people often leave them a legacy, which sets them apart from the pathetic masses.

'I am a member of the Aryan race and my family heritage is testimony to my superiority. My parents and grandparents were honored to have known the glorious leader of the Third Reich—the Fuhrer, Adolf Hitler himself. History has labeled him a criminal only because he lost. Had he been victorious, no doubt history would have judged him differently.

'In my eyes, I'm not a criminal. I have done nothing wrong and have only pursued those things which were rightfully mine. I can't be held responsible if others have suffered in the course of the fulfilment of my destiny. The path of greatness and achievement is often strewn with the bodies of those who could not meet the challenge, or those who were obstacles to great men with a sense of destiny. I have only one life to live and I have always intended to make the most of it. I'll continue to do so while there's strength in my body.'

After Kurt's tirade, Apollo voiced the following thoughts, while continuing to thrust and parry with the lighter rapier (following Kurt's gesture to change weapons). 'Kurt, I'm well aware of history and the way customs and morality do change, based on the culture of the day. However, you rationalize morality to accommodate your own desires and ambitions so that, in your mind, your despicable and ruthless means justify your selfish ends. In other words, you justify your criminality to appease what little conscience you possess.

'I concede that the culture of the day is often the arbiter of what society will deem to be morally acceptable or legal. But we're now living in the 21st century and the zeitgeist of past eras doesn't apply today. We live in a much more egalitarian and tolerant world. In thinking primarily of yourself, at the expense of others, you've overlooked that fact.

'In ancient Greece, self-willed individuals who defied the order of the gods with extreme arrogance (known as hubris) were punished with divine retribution by the goddess Nemesis. Comparatively speaking, you might regard me as your nemesis, who's come to bring you to justice.'

Each duelist, in turn, advanced towards his opponent and then stepped backwards, with both demonstrating dazzling footwork. The duel now sped up to a fever pitch, with the use of the much lighter, but equally deadly, foils. Up onto chairs, tables and desks the combatants leapt, bobbing and weaving like boxers, to avoid the potentially deadly kiss of steel from his opponent's blade.

The contestants continued their clash with amazing agility, both in attack and strategic retreat. They went from one room to another in what was developing into a monumental struggle, witnessed by the group of onlookers, which included the animals. All of the spectators sensed that the contest should proceed without interference, as there had to be a decisive conclusion to this matter of honor and principle.

Clearly, the audience expected and hoped that Apollo would be the victor, but before the swordfight ended, Apollo wanted to set Kurt straight with more well-chosen words: 'So you don't believe in absolutes, Kurt? There is no right or wrong, no good or evil. There is no crime or punishment; no heaven or hell; no God or Satan; and no judgment after death. If there is no retribution, we don't need to care about anyone but ourselves. I suppose you also believe that when we die and leave our physical body, we no longer exist.'

Kurt disdainfully replied: 'My young, naive friend, I believe only in the magic of this physical world—I don't believe there's any reward or judgment after we die. When you're dead, you're dead; you cease to exist in any form. You go back into the dust of the earth.

'My philosophy is that life is like an orange: you should squeeze as much juice out of life as possible and enjoy it while the orange is fresh and juicy, because one day it'll wither and die.'

Knowing that Kurt's knowledge of eschatology was completely lacking and that his ethical principles were unconscionable, Apollo determined to have the last word. 'There will be a day of reckoning, accountability and judgment, both in this physical existence and in the spiritual life to come. The authorities for the dispensation of justice in this world will ultimately impose punishment commensurate with your crimes. Likewise, the universal Force for Good will not be mocked. Mark my words—you will, indeed, reap what you have sown!

'In your eternal afterlife you will be judged according to your deeds in this life. You will be rewarded for your good works and held accountable for your wilful misdeeds. You will have plenty of earthly time to reflect on these matters in jail.

But remember—eternity is an infinitely longer time than *the twinkling of an eye* which is our earthly existence.'

Apollo was becoming tired of the verbal sparring with Kurt, more so than the physical duel. He could see that it would take a monumental effort to convert Kurt from his nihilistic philosophy of life. At the same time, the duel itself was becoming tedious to Apollo. Despite a facade of bravado, Kurt appeared decidedly weary.

Apollo then noticed what appeared to be a replica of the Spear of Destiny mounted on the wall behind Kurt. Also aware of it, Kurt reached for the lance in desperation, with the intention of using it against Apollo. But he was unable to grasp it and the spear fell to the ground, landing at the feet of Apollo. Still dueling with his right hand, Apollo picked up the spear with his left.

Worn out by the length of the duel, Kurt was experiencing fatigue and losing concentration and focus. Apollo knew it was time to end the contest. He lunged forward and thrust the Spear of Destiny into Kurt's right axilla (armpit). The plexus of nerves, vital blood vessels and muscles in that area were thus severely damaged rendering Kurt unable to hold his sword with his dominant hand. With his right arm essentially useless and blood pouring from his axillary wound, Kurt was totally defenseless.

Having vanquished his ultimate enemy, Apollo ironically now chose to save Kurt's life. Using some torn cloth, Apollo fashioned a compression bandage to stem the flow of blood, as there was the distinct danger that Kurt would exsanguinate before being taken into custody.

The Spear of Destiny had indeed changed Kurt's destiny, but not in the way that he would have liked. He superstitiously believed (as had the Nazis) that possession of what appeared to be the Holy Lance would give him power over his enemies. Ironically, the wound from the spear now meant his defeat at the hands of Apollo. Next would come his trial, judgement, incarceration and, hopefully, some degree of rehabilitation.

Having subdued and secured all of Kurt's henchmen and having prevented any of the foreign heads of state and other drug buyers from leaving the complex, the FBI were immediately summoned. Within minutes of notifying the FBI, the formerly impregnable fortress (now with its defenses down) was easily accessible to an army of Federal police, emergency doctors and ambulance personnel.

Apollo advised the medical team of Kurt's life-threatening wound and of the injuries of his bodyguards. All were transferred under police guard to the nearest surgical unit. The hapless drug-addicted automatons, who had been the subject of Kurt's experiments, were all transported to the closest medical unit for reversal of the effects of UXF and for treatment of their drug dependencies.

Once Kurt was apprehended, another force of FBI agents swooped on the country complex, putting the whole prison under lockdown. As previously arranged, Antonio was brought to the country prison facility by the FBI as a key witness, to expose the men who had violated his daughter.

Antonio did, indeed, identify the tall prison guard, about whom Apollo had been suspicious, as the one who had raped his daughter. He also identified that guard's accomplice in the criminal act.

The city complex had been under 24-hour surveillance since the time Apollo had extracted Damien's full confession. In fact, on Apollo's advice, the whole of the city complex had been placed in lockdown and all communication devices were disabled and rendered ineffective to prevent Kurt being alerted. The full exposé by Damien had been recorded in its entirety by Apollo for subsequent court proceedings.

As all the offenders were being rounded up by the FBI, the officer in charge of the operation at Kurt's fortress noticed the flag flying over the castle near the helicopter pad. He was particularly taken aback by the presence of some of the symbolism on it and asked Apollo: 'What's that flag? It's got that outdated symbol in the corner; that's an affront to our country. It's a slap in the face of the free world!'

'That flag bears the Von Grimmelhoff family crest,' replied Apollo. 'I believe Kurt modified the original design. Whatever way you look at it, I agree … it's totally inappropriate to fly that banner in "the land of the free and the home of the brave".'

Apollo reflected with sadness: 'When I remember all those fine boys who sacrificed their lives to keep this country free for future generations of Americans … well, it just it makes my blood boil to see such a flag flying in the USA. I just happen to have "Old Glory" with me—so with the permission of the FBI, I'll remove that flag and replace it with the "Stars and Stripes". It'll bring back memories of the flag raising on Iwo Jima in 45.'

'Bring back memories, you say—you weren't even born then!' chuckled the much older-looking FBI agent. 'But I agree—today, we've triumphed, on a major scale, over an all-pervasive criminal organization … thanks mainly to you, young fella. It's only fitting that you be the one to raise our country's flag in place of the other.'

With that endorsement from the FBI officer, Apollo proceeded with the flag raising ceremony. As he did so, Apollo found that he had attracted an audience of supporters in the form of his woodland friends. All of those wonderful creatures who had played a part in this most important victory now formed a circle around Apollo in a demonstration of reverence and respect not usually associated with wild creatures.

As Apollo raised the flag in honor of fallen comrades from bygone days, his eyes welled up as he recalled with crystal clarity, battles fought together as brothers-in-arms. As the strains of the Marines' Hymn echoed in his ears, a solitary tear of nostalgia, mixed with joy, trickled down his cheek. (See copy of Marines' Hymn in Appendix 6.)

When the flag was fully raised, Apollo's old friend the bald eagle swooped down from the blue to land on the top of the flag pole, flapping his wings in a gesture of elation and solidarity for the victory that had been achieved.

For one brief moment, rubbing his eyes in disbelief, Apollo was astonished to see the winged figure of the goddess of victory, Nike, flying overhead in her chariot. He looked a second time, but she had disappeared into the ether, as gods are wont to do. With a quizzical look on his face, Apollo wondered whether it may have been an angelic being sent by the Force for Good, to acknowledge and applaud his momentous victory.

The illegal immigrants who had been duped into entering the country—such as Antonio, Carmen and their children— were advised that they would be absolved of any wrongdoing, especially if they cooperated in giving evidence. Much to their relief, they were reassured that they would all be given an opportunity to become US citizens.

Fortunately, Fernando made a full recovery from his drug-induced brush with death. He is now on the road to complete drug rehabilitation. The test subjects who survived the diabolical UXF drug experiment are now receiving optimum medical care, through the auspices of the US government. They are all showing steady signs of improvement.

With the arrest of Kurt and his cohorts, it was inevitable that the foundations of his evil and destructive empire would start to disintegrate and eventually collapse. All those men, women and children who had been held in subjugation and fear by the tentacles of his monstrous, octopus-like organisation would now be free to return to their families and homes. Resumption of a normal life without apprehension and intimidation was now a real possibility for so many. Parents, whose children were in the grip of addiction to illicit drugs, could now breathe a sigh of relief in the knowledge that a major enemy in the war on drugs had been eliminated.

Chapter 34
Auld Lang Syne

After all that had transpired, Apollo thought it was time to pay his respects to some old comrades-in-arms for 'auld lang syne', so he made his way down to Arlington National Cemetery. Just before reaching Arlington, he decided to take a sobering look at one of the private cemeteries in the vicinity. In the warmth of the late-morning sun and without a breath of wind, the atmosphere pervading the cemetery was one of serenity and deep reverence.

As he entered the grounds of the private cemetery, Apollo noticed a young lady who, from a side view, conjured up memories of someone he had once known. She was placing flowers on a relatively new and well-maintained grave. The young girl, with her mournful demeanor and crestfallen countenance, exhibited all the signs of someone recently bereaved.

Although he would not usually have approached a grieving relative at a cemetery, Apollo was fascinated by an extraordinary collection of doves and swallows surrounding her. His curiosity was strongly aroused by the multitude of birds, and he was irresistibly drawn towards the girl and the grave site. Could this be a sign from Aphrodite, thought his ancient Greek spirit? Deep in thought, the young girl seemed unaware of her feathered admirers.

As Apollo drew closer to the young lady, he politely greeted her with a softly spoken 'hello' and a word of condolence. In response, she slowly turned towards him. As their eyes met, Apollo could not believe what he saw. He gazed at her for an inappropriately long time, transfixed by her face. She returned his gaze but with a contemplative look, indicating that she was trying to work out if she knew Apollo. She then turned away in order to rearrange the flowers on the grave and politely replied: 'Thank you. Did you know my grandmother?'

In an attempt to answer the question, Apollo looked at the headstone which read: *In loving memory of our beloved mother and grandmother, Sandra Jones (nee Cooper). Born 4 July 1921, died 1 November 2016, aged 95 years*. Apollo immediately knew to whom the grave was dedicated; but it was impossible to explain that to the young lady. He therefore replied, 'No ... I didn't know your grandmother, but I'm sure she was a wonderful lady.'

'Thank you for saying that,' the girl replied. 'Even though I'm only 25 years old, my whole life was spent with her and, in many ways, she was closer to me than my own mother. I'm going to miss her so much.' The girl was scarcely able to hold back her tears.

Embracing the opportunity to share her loss and unburden herself of the onerous weight of her grief, the girl continued to pour out her heart to Apollo. 'Grandma Sandra was my father's mother. She was a registered nurse during World War Two and continued to work as a nurse until her early seventies. My grandmother inspired me to become a nurse also. I'm now qualified as a registered nurse and I really enjoy taking care of people, just as she did. By the way, my name is Helen.'

Apollo responded politely: 'I'm delighted to meet you Helen, though I wish it could have been under happier circumstances. My name is Apollo.'

Apollo could see by the change in her demeanor that Helen was relishing the opportunity to speak to him. In order to convey his continuing interest in her grandmother's life story, Apollo took the liberty of sitting down on a nearby park bench and asked: 'Did your grandmother have a happy life?'

Helen reflected for a brief moment, then sat down on the other end of the bench and responded, 'All things considered, she did have a very happy life, but ...' She paused for a further moment, probably wondering whether it was appropriate to discuss further personal details about her beloved grandmother with someone she had just met.

Curious for further information, Apollo prompted her by asking: 'But ... was there something more you wanted to say?'

Helen again paused, took a deep breath and locked her eyes onto Apollo with an intense gaze. She gave him the impression that she regarded him as an honest and inoffensive stranger to whom she could confide information which she had been bursting to tell someone for a long time. 'You know ...' she said, hesitating momentarily before going on, 'you know, my grandmother loved my grandfather and they were very happy together. But, after he passed away— several years ago now, she took me aside one day for a deep and heartfelt talk. My grandmother confided information about her life during the war which she had never discussed with her husband, her son or anyone else.

'I was the only one that she was prepared to confide in, concerning her innermost feelings. Perhaps it was because we had grown so close to each other and I was a female.

'I'm not really sure why I'm discussing these personal family matters with you, but I guess it's because you are an impartial outsider. I suppose it's like unburdening oneself to a counselor, psychologist or priest, knowing that what is spoken in confidence will never be divulged. Although … it probably doesn't really matter anymore, because they have both passed on to their greater reward, as they say.

'Apparently, my grandmother was planning to marry a Marine Sergeant in 1945 but, before they had a chance to marry, he was killed at Iwo Jima. She confided to me that, despite the passage of time, she'd never gotten over losing him and that he was the only man that she ever really loved. But she knew that she had to move on. Otherwise, she would've lived her life like a lonely, grieving widow, bereft of any family.

'My grandmother said that the year she spent with him before his death on the battlefield was the most precious year of her life … and that never changed till the day she died. Obviously this topic could never be discussed with my grandfather, but finally she was able to unburden herself to me, when the time was right and no-one's feelings could be hurt by such a revelation.

'Grandma had kept mementos and keepsakes including cards, letters and the vinyl records they had listened to together. She'd kept them secretively from my grandfather, because she didn't have the heart to dispose of them; but, at the same time, she didn't want to hurt my grandfather by revealing them to him. Grandma left all these possessions to me. They now hold pride of place in a special cupboard in my home.

'The only things she didn't have were photographs of her Sergeant—something to do with *security reasons*. Some photos she took herself were either lost or destroyed. So, I don't really know what he looked like, but she told me he was very handsome with a great physique. More importantly— Grandma said he was a kind, loving and wonderful gentleman.

'I really do like those old Frank Sinatra records from the 1940s. I guess I'm an old-fashioned girl at heart. The record she especially loved—and I do too—was *This Love of Mine*. That was apparently their favorite.'

Feeling that she had been talking too much, Helen looked at her watch and exclaimed, 'Hey, look at the time! Sorry for boring you for so long. I really must be going, but I didn't catch your full name.'

Before providing his full name, Apollo quickly countered with a question, asking Helen the name of her grandmother's wartime fiancé. Helen replied without hesitation: 'His name was United States Marine Sgt. Peter Power. I've got all of his cards and notes, including the letter he'd written to my grandma on Iwo Jima. He died before it could be sent to her. One of his Marine buddies delivered it in person to her with the grim news of his death. Reading the letter, it sounded as though he had a premonition that he wouldn't return'.

'Why do you say that?' queried Apollo.

'Because of the last words in his letter. I've read the letter so many times that I can quote them exactly: *Whatever happens to me, wherever I may be, I will always love you, my darling, throughout eternity*. Beautiful words ... but so prophetic and tragic, as it turned out.'

'Indeed, living without the love of your life and dying prematurely are very tragic events—if that's the end of life with nothing to follow. But I have a strong feeling that there's more to our existence than people know,' Apollo replied, with a sense of confidence that Helen found mysterious, but reassuring.

With a glint in his eye and a radiant smile, Apollo then held out his hand as a gesture of friendship and said: 'Helen, my full name is Apollo Rhodes. My parents named me after the Greek god, Apollo, because they both had a keen interest in Greek mythology. Now that we've been formally introduced, I'd like an opportunity to get to know to you better. May I give you my address and cell phone number? And if possible, I'd also like to have your phone number and address.'

'Of course' she replied. 'I think I really would like to know you better, Apollo. I must say... I do like that name.'

As he spoke to Helen, Apollo marveled at how closely she physically resembled her dear departed grandmother, who he had loved so passionately. In fact, with the ever-increasing clarity of his past Spartan life, Apollo could now see that Helen also bore a striking resemblance to Amara. Apollo pondered: could it be...that Amara and either Sandra or Helen have been part of one spirit continuum? Helen's personality, her mannerisms, her voice and her way of speaking were so similar to his beloved Sandra. Likewise, he could now see similarities with Amara.

Through his physical death, Apollo had passed to the next world where loss, grief and sorrow are unknown—only light and all-pervasive love. Unfortunately, poor Sandra had been left behind to suffer in her grief, as had Amara.

During a brief pause in their conversation, during which both seemed to be reflecting on each other, a young boy of about ten years of age walked towards them and placed his right arm around Helen's shoulder. 'Hi Bobby,' Helen greeted the cute little fellow. 'Apollo, this is my nephew, Bobby—he came with me today. Bobby, this is Mr. Apollo Rhodes.'

'Hi, Mr. Rhodes, pleased to meet you, 'declared the boy, with exceptional politeness for his tender years.

'You're a very courteous young man, Bobby. I must say that I'm very pleased to meet you also,' replied Apollo.

'Hey, Mr. Rhodes, what happens to people like my great-grandma when they die and get buried in the ground?'

'Bobby, it's not fair to ask such a question of someone you've just met,' interrupted Helen.

'Helen, that's okay,' interjected Apollo, 'I'd like to answer the question.' Apollo paused for a moment then squatted down to engage the boy, eye to eye.

'Bobby, I want you to know, beyond a shadow of a doubt, that your great-grandmother has gone to a wonderful place, full of love, peace and contentment. It's a magnificent place called Heaven. The ancient Greeks called it the Elysian Fields. Some of our Native American brothers called it 'the high ground', where everything they ever wanted in their physical lives was available in abundance when they passed over. Whatever you want to call it, just know that it's an awesome and majestic place— our physical brains just cannot imagine how good it is!

'Know also that in that heavenly place there are no more tears, no more sorrow, no sickness and no pain. It's a place where time means nothing and life goes on forever. It's a wonderfully exciting and fulfilling life, where nothing is boring and everything is fun. In Heaven, there's no more war and no bad feelings—just love and goodwill for one another. It's where we live as spirits—it's our spiritual home. We humans are spirit beings living in a physical body; but we're really more spirit than physical creatures.

'If you think of the best and happiest day you've ever had in your whole life, it's like that. Every day is like that in Heaven. Another good thing is that we get to see all of our loved ones and friends who've passed over—whenever we like, for as long as we like.

'This may be a little hard for you to understand at your age, Bobby. Just know that your great-grandma and anyone else you've ever loved who's died, are now happy in their heavenly home—beyond anything that you can imagine.'

'Wow, Mr. Rhodes, that sounds great! I'm really glad great-grandma is so happy and having a lot of fun. But I'm happy too and having a lot of fun right now,' declared Bobby.

'I'm glad you're happy, Bobby. All little boys and girls should be happy and have fun. Above all, they should be loved and, if I'm as good a judge as I think I am, I would say that you're greatly loved,' replied Apollo.

Not fully understanding all that Apollo had said, but satisfied by what he'd been told, Bobby skipped away, his attention distracted by some colorful butterflies he had spotted.

'Thank you for answering my young nephew's question in such an optimistic and descriptive manner. Children are so trusting and will often believe whatever adults tell them,' commented Helen, after pulling Apollo out of earshot of Bobby.

'I agree,' replied Apollo, 'that's why it's always important to tell them the truth, which I did. One day, when we get to know each other better, I'll explain to you more about the truth, as I know it.'

Not quite knowing what to make of what Apollo had just said, Helen simply replied 'Okay', with a puzzled look on her face.

Helen was clearly impressed by Apollo's general manner and the kindness and concern with which he had addressed her and her nephew. She also couldn't help but admire his youthful good looks and impressive physique. Helen had decided in her own mind that she would like to cultivate a friendship, perhaps even pursue a relationship, with this outstanding young man.

They exchanged details before parting that day and agreed to meet at a piano recital which Helen was looking forward to attending. Until now, she hadn't organized a friend to go with her.

CHAPTER 35
LOST AND FOUND

After his chance meeting with Helen, Apollo carried out his intended pilgrimage to Arlington. Before he was struck by lightning, Arlington meant nothing to Apollo personally. He just knew it as an historical graveyard for the military. Now it meant everything to him. As he walked slowly and solemnly past the myriad gravestones, a name would catch his attention and rekindle cherished memories of comradeship in battle and good times spent with buddies. He then wondered for a moment where the physical remains of Peter Power might be—he did not see the name on any headstone or plaque. He dismissed the thought from his mind for the moment.

After his emotional reunion with departed friends Apollo decided it was time to rest. He then returned to the privacy and seclusion of his apartment and reflected on the momentous events that had recently transpired to transform his life.

In recent days, he had performed great feats of heroism, physical strength and tactical skills that would have made both his Spartan comrades and his Marine Corps buddies proud. He had all but single-handedly vanquished the oppressive and destructive empire of a nefarious drug lord, whose despicable crimes had rarely been perpetrated by other criminals. Apollo had freed many souls from slavery and oppression under Von Grimmelhoff's evil influence.

Apollo was astonished to think that, serendipitously, the young woman he had just met was the grand-daughter of Sandra, the love of his World War Two life. More amazingly, he was beginning to think that Helen might be the embodiment of the spirit of his Spartan wife, Amara, which prophetically means 'eternal'.

His other thought was that Sandra may actually have been the physical receptacle of Amara's spirit. All three women shared so many similarities of which Apollo alone had knowledge. It seemed unbelievable, but Apollo had learnt from personal experience that the unimaginable and incredible can sometimes become real and tangible.

Apollo's mind was racing. He sensed that his brainpower was expanding further in some indefinable way. Then the ringing of the phone interrupted his train of thought. It was Apollo's mother, Maria Rhodes. 'Son, I haven't seen you for a while. What've you been up to? Are you well? I've been so worried about you since the lightning strike and then ... that assault.'

'Sure Ma, I'm fine. I've been meaning to come and see you, but I've been indisposed, you might say, with official business. But that job's over ... so I'll be able to spend more time with you from now on. Is there anything you need me to help you with?'

'No son, I don't need any help at the moment, but there is one thing. Do you remember that day, when I was sick, just before the lightning accident? I told you there were things that I'd misplaced, relating to your father. Well, I found something that I'd like you to see. It's ...' Maria paused for a few seconds, in an attempt to hold back her tears. 'It's a videotape your father made a week before he died. Would you like to come over and look at it tonight?'

'Sure Ma. I'd really like to see it. I'll drop over tonight. See you then. Love you ma—big time.'

'Love you too, son. Bye.'

That night Apollo walked into his mother's living room to view the long-lost video with a strong sense of anticipation. He recalled what a wonderful and caring man his father, Phillip Rhodes, had been. Much to his regret and displeasure, Apollo's father had often deprived himself of his family's company to work for their ultimate financial benefit.

With tears streaming down his face, Apollo hung on every word uttered by his father in the video. It was filmed in his final days, and he was gaunt, pale and emaciated—a shadow of his former, vibrant self. Apollo listened intently as his dear departed father lamented with indignation that life was too short.

Apollo's father addressed him directly by name in this his valedictory speech: 'Just when a man feels he's getting somewhere, it's time to retire, because some young upstart is breathing down your neck. Then your boss decides that *you're gettin' too old for the job* or, worse still, the big C (cancer) comes out of left field to sock you in the pit of your stomach, stomp on your head and kick you in the teeth when you're down.'

He continued poignantly, in a frustrated and quivering voice and with a lugubrious expression on his face: 'One life isn't enough for a man to achieve what he wants. It's not enough to do and enjoy what he desires in his deepest dreams. Life's too short to learn and experience what's needed to live a fulfilled life. There are so many things that have been left undone. There are so many words of love, kindness and encouragement that will remain unspoken, and so many wonderful songs of joy that will go unsung. My precious son, I love you more than my own life, and I only want the best for you,' he declared unequivocally.

Phillip Rhodes exhorted his son: 'Cram as much as you can into your life. Live life to the full. Make the most of it, because you have only one life to live. But, above all, hug your family and your loved ones. Be kind and understanding to those around you, even though they may not show the same kindness to you. Acts of love and goodwill to others carry their own rewards for the giver— reciprocation is welcomed, but not necessary.

'Apollo, my boy, just remember—when your number is up—it's how many people you've helped in your life, not the dollars in your bank account, that will earn you the most respect, honor and eternal glory.

'Goodbye, my son. I love you ... I'll see you on the other side.' There the video ended, with Phillip Rhodes exhausted and the signs of impending death becoming more evident.

Apollo was convinced that his wonderful dad was right in every point he made. Apollo fully intended to make his present earthly life count to the maximum achievable level, for the good of others and consequently for his own good. Notwithstanding agreement with his father's sentiments, Apollo acknowledged to himself that he'd been peculiarly blessed. He now had vivid, tangible memories of his past lives—he could use them to build his present life, to levels that would be unachievable without the foundation provided by his many previous years of life on earth.

Apollo's tears of sadness at remembering his father's suffering and agonizing death were now tempered by joy derived from the certain knowledge that they would eventually be reunited in an eternal life of perpetual bliss. Moreover, Apollo felt great comfort in knowing that their heavenly life would be unfettered by the stresses and constraints of time, aging and infirmity which can so onerously shackle people in their physical existence.

CHAPTER 36
THE PIANO RECITAL

It was the night of the piano recital. Apollo had mentioned to his mother that he was attending with a wonderful girl he had just met. Knowing his mother had an appreciation of classical music, he had invited her to join them. The theme for the night was piano pieces by Beethoven. Several works of Beethoven were played by a number of accomplished pianists. However, when it came time to play one of the master's greatest pieces, the designated pianist was found to be ill and unable to perform at the last minute.

The organizer of the evening, in an attempt to encourage audience participation, made an impromptu request for a member of the audience to give their rendition of Beethoven's *Fur Elise*. The audience members looked around to see if anyone would respond to the invitation at such short notice. When it appeared that no-one was courageous enough to perform in front of several hundred people, Apollo decided to raise his hand. But before doing so, he whispered to Helen: 'I'll show them how the maestro himself would've executed this piece, and one day, when the time is right, I'll tell you how I know.'

What followed was perhaps the most outstanding and impressive rendition of Beethoven's *Fur Elise* that had ever been heard in that music hall, much to the acclaim of the veteran pianists and conductors fortuitously in attendance on that particular night.

At the end of the performance, Helen remarked to Apollo's mother: 'Mrs. Rhodes, your son is an excellent pianist. You obviously invested a lot of time and money in arranging piano lessons for him when he was a boy. You must be very proud of him.'

Maria Rhodes nodded in bewilderment, but she was too dumbstruck to respond. Maria was flabbergasted at Apollo's flawless and professional performance. She knew full well that he had never received a music lesson of any kind in his life!

Kindled by yet another remarkable facet to Apollo's repertoire of diverse talents, so began the relationship between Apollo and Helen. The details will provide a story for another day!

EPILOGUE

Recorded by Tommy Dorsey and Frank Sinatra in 1941, the song *This Love of Mine* concludes with the words: *this love of mine goes on*. Where does love go when we or our loved ones no longer exist in this physical world? It goes on—in the next world. Our love for each other—if it is true, honest and unselfish—lives on, long after our earthly bodies have vanished in the dust of time. Such love, like the spirit of man, is unquenchable and immortal.

Even the experts in neuroscience and neurosurgery agree that we have only begun to plumb the depths of the human brain. We are still only in the infancy of our understanding of the mind of man. We are just seeing the tip of the iceberg. We know considerably less about the human spirit and the spiritual forces pervading our world.

Have we all lived before? Have we all loved before? Even though we may fantasize that we have, none of us knows with any certainty—we simply do not have the proof. Only one man, our hero, Apollo Rhodes, can claim such a distinction. The story you have read is his testimony. And there is more to come—much more!

A Special Note from the Author — The Wisdom of Apollo Rhodes

Apollo Rhodes is in the unique position of possessing the wisdom, knowledge and understanding of life (and death) that can only be acquired from centuries of spirit-man living. He has the benefit of insights directly obtained from the ancient Greek philosophers and the oracles of the ancient gods of Olympus. Apollo also has arcane knowledge derived from first-hand interaction with some of the most famous, revered and intellectually elite figures of all time—Benjamin Franklin and Mozart, to name but two.

As a modern American youth, Apollo Rhodes is also able to blend the zeitgeist and scientific advancements of our 21st century world with his centuries of spirit-man wisdom, to formulate foundational principles for successful and happier living in today's uncertain world.

Please read on to discover Apollo Rhodes' Seven Pillars of Ancient Wisdom and his Seven Golden Nuggets of Modern Wisdom.

THE SEVEN PILLARS
OF ANCIENT WISDOM

The Seven Pillars of Ancient Wisdom, on which strong foundations for successful lives can be built, are sage wisdom from the ancient gods, their oracles and the Greek philosophers:

1. When you are overwhelmed by the humiliation of defeat on the battlefield of life, be not dismayed—remain undaunted. Do not indulge in self-pity or self-flagellation. Identify your errors and learn from your painful experience. Regroup and return to the arena with renewed strength and new hope. So re-armed, the final and lasting victory will be within your grasp.

2. Ultimately, it is not where you start or where you have been, but how and where you finish that will be recorded on your epitaph and by which posterity and history will remember you.

3. It is often those eventualities which you least expect to materialize that may be your ultimate undoing. Do not discount unlikely contingencies as folly, but be mindful of them. Reflect upon such things and prepare for and against them, so that they will not be left as a legacy to torment or haunt you throughout your remaining days.

4. Inevitably there will be circumstances that can never be controlled. You must seek the wisdom, guidance and the beneficence of the gods to overcome such unforeseen challenges and crises, if and when they suddenly appear. In order to receive the assistance of the gods, appropriate supplication and penance will assuredly be demanded and required by them.

5. Time can be your enemy or your friend—it depends on how you use it. Patience and perseverance with realistic optimism are virtuous attributes required for success. Headstrong impetuosity is the downfall of many a good man.

6. Hubris (arrogance before the gods) is the worst of crimes against the immortal powers and demands that Nemesis—the punisher and the dispenser of implacable justice—administer retribution. It is the humble man—the one who respects the divinity of the gods—who will receive the invaluable and essential mercy and magnanimity of the gods, thus affording him the achievement of victory in life.

7. In the competition of life, it is not the idle man who succeeds, but the one who consistently does what the average man is not prepared to do. It is the ancient law of sowing and reaping. If you sow nothing, you harvest nothing. If you sow goodness, you reap more goodness. If you disseminate evil, it will inexorably return to destroy you like a flood. When mortal man takes his final breath, it is hoped that his life will be remembered as one well lived, with few or no regrets. And if the contribution of his life to his generation is great enough, his legacy will be celebrated and glorified for centuries or millennia thereafter.

THE SEVEN GOLDEN NUGGETS OF MODERN WISDOM

The Seven Golden Nuggets of Modern Wisdom come from centuries of spirit-man wisdom:

1. Let not our beliefs divide us. Let our beliefs— though they be different—draw us closer to each other by virtue of their positive commonalities.

2. Respect all forms of life and, as much as possible, help maintain the natural ecological balance of nature.

3. Believe in the higher Force for Good towards which you can set your moral compass—by so doing you can be assured that your life force is flowing in the right direction. You become what you aspire to and worship.

4. It is incumbent on every human being to give back to the world at least to the extent that they have received from the world. The more one has been privileged to receive, the more it is expected that one will give back in return. Express daily gratitude for your life's blessings, however small, and they will be multiplied unto you.

5. Take every opportunity to encourage and uplift those you meet—never belittle others; you will in turn be exalted in their eyes. Leave a legacy from which future generations will benefit and by which the memory of your life will never fade. In so doing your immortality will be assured.

6. The physical life is short and full of distractions, minefields, pitfalls and dead-ends. They can be

avoided and success can be assured, but only through determined focus on specific objectives.

7. Never be ashamed of or feel inferior about who you are, or where you have come from. None of us is the same—we are all unique and special in our own way. Each of us has a talent or a quality that can be utilized for the benefit of ourselves and others. So find it, and start using it!

APPENDIX I
THE PHENOMENAL AND
MYSTERIOUS HUMAN BRAIN

Even in this day and age, the brain of man remains a mysterious and unfathomable organ. The general public thinks that doctors and medical scientists know everything there is to know about the human brain. But even medical researchers are constantly surprised by the marvels it can perform, many of which defy logic. In fact, in a recent interview with a number of neurosurgeons, the consensus of opinion was that we have only touched the proverbial 'tip of the iceberg' when it comes to understanding the brain and all of its underlying functions. Sure, we understand the anatomy, but we are still learning about the functions and the interconnections between the numerous areas of the brain that we can identify.

The term 'neuroplasticity' is commonly used to describe the way in which the brain is malleable or moldable like plastic and can be reshaped and improved. It was once thought that the number of brain cells (neurons) and their interconnections (synapses) diminished with age. This is true to a degree, as humans slow down with aging, but it is now understood that neuro-regeneration (creation of new brain cells) is possible with mental stimulation. New brain pathways can be set down where old ones have been damaged by injury. This is particularly so with those areas of the brain that are responsible for memory and emotions, such as the hippocampus and the amygdala.

It is less than a hundred years since the invention of the computer as we know it today. Yet our brains, under unique and diverse circumstances, can make man-made computers appear inferior by comparison. It is sadly true that the vast majority of humans live their all too short and unfulfilled lives with mysteries and treasures locked inside their brain. They stay buried like the ancient treasures of Egypt or other long-lost civilizations

It is often said that we use only 10% of our brain capacity, but this is an urban myth and has become somewhat of a cliché. Nevertheless, it is true that we have the capacity to harness our brains to achieve far more than we imagine.

Regrettably, all too often, the potentially magnificent and awe-inspiring symphony of our lives is never heard, because the music box of our hearts and souls is never opened. As much as we try, our purposeful and deliberate efforts to learn more, to understand more, to achieve more and to become more are often in vain.

It is possible, however, for the inscrutable hand of fate to unexpectedly (and often suddenly and dramatically) enter and transform our sometimes desperate, unfulfilled, and sadly mundane lives. We may then realize the full potential of our being and the unlimited capacity of our brains to see visions and know worlds that we could never have imagined otherwise.

The Amazing Mind of Man

Who can explain the phenomenon of the autistic savant (formerly called the "idiot savant" syndrome), now often called the savant syndrome? It describes someone with a mental disability who, in other areas—such as calculation, memory or musical skills—far exceeds the average ability of so-called normal people. We can document its existence. We can witness it, and testify to it, and describe it in action in the lives of the savants, but we do not fully understand it. This phenomenon is usually an accident of birth, but it may be acquired, and we have no understanding of its causation. We merely stand in awe and marvel at the phenomenal and inexplicable abilities demonstrated by the savant. Such unique and focused talents are unfortunately at the expense and sacrifice of other pedestrian faculties that we average human beings take for granted. It has been postulated that the savant syndrome may arise from some damage to the left anterior temporal lobe of the brain.

Medical scientists describe children with autism and Asperger's syndrome in a similar way, but we do not understand the whys and wherefores of these conditions. Recent studies have shown that autistic children and adults may not be lacking in intelligence at all. They may actually be more intelligent than the so-called 'normal' person. Even so, they are unfortunate prisoners of a world where their ability to communicate is impaired. This is because they are functioning, on a daily basis, from a different perspective or in a 'parallel dimension', where the key to the door (perhaps even the door itself) from one dimension to the next does not exist.

Our understanding of mental illness, although far advanced over previous eras of history, remains sadly lacking. This is true, despite the development of mind-altering drugs to seemingly restore function to unfortunate sufferers.

We still do not understand why some of history's most intellectually brilliant and accomplished men and women have been described as suffering from bipolar disorder, otherwise known as manic depressive psychosis. In this condition, to varying degrees, the sufferer vacillates between depression and different levels of euphoria known as mania or hypomania.

Some individuals of great achievement and major historical significance, such as Sir Winston Churchill, have suffered from major depression. Churchill metaphorically compared or likened his bouts of depression to a 'black dog'. The Black Dog Institute (one of the world's leading medical institutions for the treatment of depression and mood disorders) was named after Churchill's 'black dog'. It is somewhat disconcerting to surmise that Churchill may have made his most profound and momentous decisions, on behalf of the free world, at times when his mental faculties had become bound by the shackles of depressed thinking.

AFTER DEATH: WHAT THEN?

We do not really understand life after death experiences (the so-called white light and tunnel phenomenon), but the frequency with which such experiences have been and continue to be reported testifies to the strong likelihood that we are more than just physical beings. The so-called 'out of body experience' described by many cannot be dismissed as mere hallucination or fabrication. In the course of a reduced level of physical consciousness, such as experienced with a cardiac arrest, the subject of lost consciousness seemingly observes everything that is going on in the ER, from the vantage point of their spirit being. Reports from those involved in such incidents are strongly suggestive of the fact that these individuals must have observed and listened to all that was happening around them through their spirit being, as the facts and details related by the subjects are too accurate to have been merely guessed or fabricated.

How often do we see a severely brain-traumatized individual, in a prolonged and profound comatose state, suddenly regain consciousness and inform the watchful family and the medical team caring for them that they were aware, but unable to communicate ? Sadly, how often in the past have comatose patients, seemingly lost to us, been given up for dead? Perhaps some were buried alive, especially in past centuries when medical understanding and technology were lacking or very primitive.

OFTEN-ASKED PUZZLING QUESTIONS ABOUT THE BRAIN OF MAN

Many other complex and vexing questions about the brain promote discussion, consultation and debate, but defy scientific explanation.

Why do some adults, even as children in their formative years, display remarkable abilities in particular areas of learning, to which they innately gravitate in terms of interest and curiosity, to the exclusion of other areas of learning in which they show little or no interest?

Some children demonstrate obvious interest in areas such as basic mechanics (Meccano sets, Lego blocks and jigsaw puzzles), electronics, computers and mathematics to the exclusion of languages, literature, music and art. And, of course, vice versa.

The broad conclusion is that the individual's brain is pre-programmed genetically with the ability to appreciate and understand specific areas of interest. It therefore gravitates to areas of human knowledge and understanding that conform to its innate make-up and view of the world.

Another interesting example of innate brain diversification is the genetic disorder known as facial blindness (prosopagnosia), where even highly accomplished, educated and intelligent individuals are unable to recognize their own faces or the faces of people that they have met previously, including their own family members. This latter condition can also be caused by traumatic injury to the brain and surprisingly occurs in one out of fifty individuals worldwide. Another surprising issue about this condition is that the sufferers do not perceive that they have a problem and hence it is rarely reported to medical practitioners!

More Questions about the Brain

How is it that some individuals are able to remember phenomenal amounts of information in certain areas of human knowledge, with little or no effort on their part, yet they are unable to understand elementary concepts in other areas of human knowledge? The reader may well be aware, through the medium of television or the internet, of those rare individuals who can recall, without error, every detail of their personal life, dating from a particular time. These people are now described as possessing "highly superior autobiographical memory"—they were formerly called "hyperthymestics" as they had hyperthymesia (literally meaning, from the Greek, "excessive remembering"). They can also recall world events reported through news media, which have occurred at a particular time of their life. They remember dates, days of the week, weather reports and minute details such as clothes worn and food eaten on a particular day. Reports of such happenings are mind-boggling and defy any simple or precise explanation.

Recent reports in the media, from established universities and other scientific institutions of learning, have documented cases of individuals who, following various forms of trauma to the brain, have experienced unusual and inexplicable changes in their abilities to perform tasks and skills which were previously beyond them. These heightened abilities and skills have also been accompanied by an intense fascination with an area that was previously of no interest, eg. playing the piano, sculpting or painting.

Another interesting phenomenon relates to the area of organ transplants, in particular heart transplants. In such situations, it is not uncommon for the organ recipient or close relatives to report that there has been a change in the recipient's personality, view of the world, interests or likes and dislikes. It is as if, along with the donor's organ, there has also been a transfer of deep-seated personality traits, brain functioning and other characteristics of the donor—a personality transplant!

Other mysteries of brain function which defy any logical scientific explanation include cases where individuals, having suffered a viral illness or other non-specific illness, no longer speak with the same accent, but with an accent entirely foreign to them and one to which they had not been exposed in earlier life. Almost the converse to this is the situation where individuals become completely amnesic following a viral illness and cannot remember their past life including any members of their family.

All of these mysterious phenomena concerning the function and neuroplasticity of the brain still puzzle the most brilliant members of the medical profession to this day.

Appendix 2

Principles of Eschatology

The views and opinions expressed here are those of the author based on the knowledge of Apollo Rhodes, gleaned over several lifetimes and after- death (heavenly) experiences. They do not specifically reflect the doctrine of any particular religion, religious affiliation or denomination.

For those who believe, no explanation is necessary. For those who do not believe, no explanation will suffice.

Most people, if they are true to themselves, will generally admit to believing in an omnipotent, omniscient and ubiquitous being that pervades our world. To some the concept is vague and amorphous; to others it may be more tangible and certain. In the English language, we use the word 'God' to represent this invisible being.

The word 'God' is used in everyday language in various ways. Insurance companies refer to 'acts of God' that cause unforeseen damage to life and property. People often talk of being saved from death or tragedy 'by the grace of God'. 'Thank God' or 'thank goodness' are frequently used expressions, to the point of cliché, when danger or disaster are averted.

For the purposes of this book, I generally refer to God as the 'Force for Good', because it is almost universally accepted that God is good and loving. I sometimes refer to him as 'the Almighty' or simply 'God'. Under his command and acting as helpers, are the Angels, meaning 'messengers'.

The realm of human spirits in the afterlife is known by most people as 'Heaven'. In Heaven all of the spirits are largely good, otherwise they would not be there. Evil spirits reside in another place called variously Hell, Hades (both the Greek god of the underworld and his domain), Tartarus (the deep abyss even deeper than the realm of Hades) or simply the Underworld. Hell does not appear to exist on the planet Earth in any geographical sense (as depicted in literary works like Dante's Inferno or as in Greek mythology). Where and in what form it exists is anybody's guess.

In Heaven, the vast majority of spirit beings reside happily in an eternal existence of light, peace, contentment and unimaginable love. The Almighty loves all of us and his love is beyond measure. In Heaven, there is no sickness, no death, no sorrow, no sadness and no pain—only well-being, fulfillment and happiness.

From the moment a person is born on Earth—that is, when he or she leaves the mother's womb and the umbilical cord is cut—the baby must start to breathe oxygen from the atmosphere. At that moment, the Spirit enters the body. The Latin word 'spirit' literally means 'to breathe in' which could be construed to mean the breath of God.

Man on Earth consists of three basic elements: a body, a spirit and a soul. The spirit can also be called the 'spirit-man' to distinguish it from the physical body that is made up of flesh and blood. The spirit-man may be male or female, depending on the gender of the physical body.

The spirit (pneuma in Greek) is what gives the body life or the ability to live, as we know it, in the earthly realm. Without the spirit, our physical bodies are just inanimate objects. You may well ask: where does the spirit, that brings life to the body, come from? The answer seems simple: the spirit comes from the 'spirit world'. But there are two spirit worlds: the realm of good spirits in Heaven and the realm of bad spirits in Hell. Both of these spirits also reside in the physical world, looking for opportunities to inhabit human beings, depending on the soul of the person.

Everyone who is born of the womb of their mother is filled with a spirit breathed into them from Almighty God. Being inspired from God, it is naturally a good and righteous spirit. God breathes life into the body, as it emerges from the womb. However, as the baby grows, this pristine, good spirit can go through change in the form of one of two basic processes (there can also be variations and degrees of change of these two processes). These processes are:

1. Maintaining and strengthening the good spirit; or

2. Gradually losing the good spirit and contaminating or even replacing it with a bad spirit, to varying degrees.

What brings about the change in the spirit is the soul of the individual; that is: the mind (the brain), the will (their choices based on God-given free will) and the emotions. The emotions are the product of the sub-conscious and the conscious mind's interpretation and response to external stimuli in the environment. Life circumstances, as well as other people with whom we are in daily contact, also determine the emotions that are elicited within us.

As the child grows, the once totally good spirit is slowly chipped away to varying degrees and at different rates by incoming evil spirits. These evil spirits are always in the earthly environment, waiting for an opportunity to gain entry into the most available or vulnerable individual. As stated, this process can only happen if, and to the extent that, a 'deteriorating' soul permits it to happen. This is what is called the process of 'losing your own soul'. A person loses his God-given good spirit-man by giving into the evil spirit forces lurking all around him in the physical world where we live. This may be a gradual and progressive process—with a regressive outcome.

Taking illegal, dangerous or hallucinatory (mind-altering) drugs such as cannabis, cocaine, speed (amphetamines) ice, ecstasy or excessive alcohol can lead to a loss of (or deterioration in) the soul. All of these excesses are tantamount to partaking of the forbidden fruit, against which mankind was warned in the beginning of human existence. Becoming involved in criminal behavior or unholy alliances with deceitful, dishonest people also leads to a deterioration in the soul.

THE FORCE FOR GOOD

It is accepted that God is invisible in the physical world, so the only way he can register his presence is in spirit form. What is referred to as the Holy Spirit in religious doctrine is the spirit of the Almighty, which is the pure essence of God (love, goodness and light) in this comparatively dark world.

The Force for Good can reside within our physical bodies at times, if we earnestly seek him and call upon him to do so. The Force for Good can stay with us along with our own spirit-man who quickened our little bodies at birth as the Almighty breathed life into us.

As a general rule, when a human being dies, their physical body turns to the dust of the earth whence it came and their spirit-man (assuming it is mostly 'good') ascends into heaven to reside there with other kindred spirits in a state of eternal peace, tranquility and contentment in the presence of the limitless love and security of the Almighty.

However, in order to explain Apollo's story, it is theorized that individuals with spirits deemed to be exceptional may be returned to Earth, to inhabit newly born infants. The choice of the returning spirit may depend upon what deeds of goodness, self-sacrifice, selflessness, courage, holiness or charity the returning spirit has performed in their lifetime. Such spirits are selected for return in order to disseminate virtue and goodness in an all-too-evil world (to even the scales). None of us would really know whether our spirit-man has dwelt in a previous body before or not. We are not really aware of our spirit-man; all we know is that we are alive and it is the spirit that gives us life.

It was only by virtue of the extremely rare event that happened to Apollo (a freak reaction of his brain to a lightning bolt that would usually kill or maim rather than enhance the brain), that a direct 'hotline' connection was set up between the memory centers of his brain and his spirit-man. Apollo was virtually able to 'download' all of his spirit-man's previous life memories into his now modified, expanded, enhanced and highly receptive current brain. His spirit had lived those lives before, even though the physical bodies that lived those experiences (which the spirit remembers) had long since turned to dust. However, based on the evidence of Apollo, the spirit-man tries to bring the physical body in line with memories of past experiences.

Another theoretical point is that when a selected spirit-man is designated for re-entry into a newly born physical body, angelic beings (the messengers from the spirit to the physical world acting only under the authority of the Almighty) will wait for a matching look-alike to arise. They can actually spot such a being in the embryonic stage of development, using their special angelic powers of surveillance and observation. The angels will thus match the incoming spirit with a person whose physical appearance, when fully mature, is extremely close to the previous 'temple'. Were they to be compared using photographic evidence (if available), it would be as if they were doppelgangers or twins.

Clearly however, although the spirit-man is living another earthly life in a new physical body (albeit a look-alike), the individual temples are not connected genealogically and therefore do not receive or pass on a name which they have inherited from an ancestor.

When he was living in Sparta in the 5th century BC, his name was Paris Apollo. When the spirit-man of Apollo returned to dwell in the 18th century temple of a German and French-speaking doppelganger (they had not linked up at that stage—no lightning bolt connection until the 21st century), his earthly name was genealogically different (it was Pierre Apollinaire—he had a French father and a German mother). There was no connection between the Greek Apollo and the Franco-German Pierre by physical lineage, but there was an even stronger and much more exact connection spirit-wise: they were one and the same spirit living at different times in the history of mankind. This was possible only because the spirit of a man lives forever—the spirit is immortal!

The catalyst that worked so well in Apollo's case, and without which he would have been totally oblivious to even the concept of past lives, was the lightning strike, which by sheer chance struck the memory centers of his brain. That part of his brain was therefore activated, stimulated and expanded far beyond anything previously seen on MRIs. Had the lightning bolt struck him only slightly differently, he may well have died on the spot or ended up a disabled vegetable. The precision with which the bolt hit could only be described as an absolute miracle.

THE SOUL

The Soul is what gives us, in a word, our 'personality'. The Soul consists of three elements:

- Firstly, the mind or our cognitive ability, which is the manifestation of the quality and integrity of our brain matter.

- Secondly, the will, which is our God-given power of choice to do right or wrong. God hopes that our choices will be guided by our good spirit-man (unfortunately some people have bad or mean spirits which do not come from God; some have, or are, 'bad seeds'). God did not make us to be robots without a will of our own and only to be controlled by what he wants. God made us choice-based, free-willed beings with whom he could have a rewarding, healthy relationship. No one wants fellowship with an automaton that only does what it is told or programmed to do—that would be very boring.

- Thirdly, our emotions. The emotional side of our soul will largely depend on the other two elements: the mind (conscious brain— how we think and interpret what is going on in the external world of our physical existence) and the will (the choices we make as free-willed human beings).

Apollo's Spirit World

Having died physically at least three times and then ascended, spiritually, into heavenly places, Apollo was aware of the reality of the afterlife. He knew that spirits communicated gloriously and happily with each other in the spirit world. He also realized that the Good Spirit, who reigns supremely and benevolently in heaven, is ubiquitous and so resides symbiotically with the spirit that filled his earthly body. In this state of symbiosis, Apollo was beginning to realize that the Good Spirit was often communicating with his soul (his mind, will and emotions). It was directing him in his own life and also prompting him (or more precisely prompting his soul) to impart profound and beneficial information to others for their betterment. Apollo called these 'promptings of the Good Spirit', which he often experienced. He had initially paid no heed to them, but eventually realized the importance of such promptings. Some people might call these 'workings of the conscience'.

We all have a conscience, which helps us differ-entiate right from wrong or good behavior from bad behavior. Some individuals are said to have 'no conscience', which means that they have no qualms or scruples when it comes to their behavior or their treatment of others. They tend to be selfish, self-in-dulgent and antisocial. Clearly, such people do not receive promptings from the Good Spirit, because they are not receptive. Indeed, such people often become criminals.

APPENDIX 3
THE GREEK GOD APOLLO
AND THE SPARTANS

(AS EXPLAINED BY APOLLO RHODES
— PREVIOUSLY KNOWN AS PARIS APOLLO)

My namesake, the god Apollo, was the patron of the Oracle at Delphi, supposedly the center of the known world. The name of the high priestess of the temple of Apollo was Pythia. Hence, it was also called the Pythian Oracle. She gave her pronouncements under the inspiration of Apollo, the god (among other things) of prophesy, knowledge and enlightenment.

The name of Delphi (which means dolphin—further derived from its meaning as "womb") was originally Pytho, named after the great serpent, Python, which Apollo slew with his bow and arrows. The Python was spawned from Gaea (Mother Earth). The monstrous snake (sometimes called a she-dragon) had been designated by Gaea to guard the Oracle.

Apart from Ares, the god of war, Apollo was the most revered god of the Spartans. Every four years, Delphi hosted the Pythian Games—second only to the ancient Olympic Games.

The Spartans respected wolves for their cunning, ferocity and their pack mentality. Apollo was thought to dwell among wolves at times, as he watched over the Spartan people. Among several titles which were given to Apollo, as epithets, was Lyceus, meaning 'guide of the wolves'. The name of Lycurgus, the original lawgiver of the Spartans, means 'protector from wolves'. He also consulted the Oracle to ask about the organization of the Spartan nation.

Apollo was the patron god of healing, but he could also bring a plague upon those who displeased him. His son was Asclepius, god of medicine, health, healing, rejuvenation and physicians. Apollo had a twin sister, Artemis, born of Leto, by Zeus, the king of the Olympian gods. Leto was the daughter of the Titans, Coeus and Phoebe.

Apollo was the god of music and was known to play the stringed instrument, the lyre. He was also god of the sun and was associated with ravens and crows, which were considered good luck. They were sometimes used by the gods as messengers to mortals. Ravens are also mentioned in the Bible where they are often seen as friends of mankind.

Many Spartans and other Greeks journeyed to the Oracle at Delphi to seek knowledge about their future or when making decisions. One of the standard maxims of the Oracle was: *know thyself.*

APPENDIX 4
MESMER AND ANIMAL MAGNETISM

It should be unambiguously understood that the modern use of the phrase 'animal magnetism', to mean sex appeal, does not form part of the original definition.

Many animals have senses, innate instincts and abilities that far exceed those of humans and which leave us perplexed and mystified at their amazing accuracy. Dogs, for example, can sense emotions and characteristics in humans that are undetectable by people.

In human beings, dogs can sense fear, diffidence, and emotional weakness (negative emotions). Conversely, they can detect fearlessness, confidence and emotional strength (positive emotions). Various species of animals will generally respond to the former negative human emotions with aggression and dominant behavior. By the same token, they will respond to the positive human emotions with passivity and submissive behavior.

Dogs have been shown to be capable of detecting disease such as cancer, diabetes and epilepsy in human beings. Such abilities are beyond human comprehension, but could be attributed to their extremely heightened five senses or to a sixth sense that could be described as animal magnetism, for want of a better description. Perhaps it could be a combination of both.

Studies have also shown that growth in some plants may be enhanced or retarded by their exposure to different kinds of music. Surely this must be an example of animal or, in this case, 'plant' magnetism!

In fact, Mesmer may have been the first to heal others by what we have now come to know as hypnotherapy, ie. therapy using hypnosis. Hypnosis is simply reaching the subconscious mind with positive, health giving suggestions. These can be either autosuggestions, as in 'self-hypnosis', or external suggestions from the hypnotherapist, while the individual is in a heightened state of receptivity. The person receiving the suggestions would be described as being 'mesmerized' or in a trancelike or highly focused state. Such suggestions implanted firmly in the subconscious mind could be expected to manifest themselves in the individual's conscious existence, thereby improving their life both emotionally and physically, depending on the suggestions implanted. Such communication between the minds of individuals certainly formed part of the definition of what Mesmer called 'animal magnetism'.

Appendix 5
The Hippocratic Oath
(Classic Version)

I swear by Apollo Physician and Asclepius and Hygieia and Panaceia and all the gods and goddesses, making them my witnesses, that I will fulfil according to my ability and judgment this oath and this covenant:

To hold him who has taught me this art as equal to my parents and to live my life in partnership with him, and if he is in need of money to give him a share of mine, and to regard his offspring as equal to my brothers in male lineage and to teach them this art - if they desire to learn it - without fee and covenant; to give a share of precepts and oral instruction and all the other learning to my sons and to the sons of him who has instructed me and to pupils who have signed the covenant and have taken an oath according to the medical law, but no-one else.

I will apply dietetic measures for the benefit of the sick according to my ability and judgment; I will keep them from harm and injustice.

I will neither give a deadly drug to anybody who asked for it, nor will I make a suggestion to this effect. Similarly, I will not give to a woman an abortive remedy. In purity and holiness, I will guard my life and my art.

I will not use the knife, not even on sufferers from stone, but will withdraw in favor of such men as are engaged in this work.

Whatever houses I may visit, I will come for the benefit of the sick, remaining free of all intentional injustice, of all mischief and in particular of sexual relations with both female and male persons, be they free or slaves.

What I may see or hear in the course of the treatment or even outside of the treatment in regard to the life of men, which on no account one must spread abroad, I will keep to myself, holding such things shameful to be spoken about.

If I fulfil this oath and do not violate it, may it be granted to me to enjoy life and art, being honored with fame among all men for all time to come; if I transgress it and swear falsely, may the opposite of all this be my lot.

Appendix 6
The Marines' Hymn

From the Halls of Montezuma
To the shores of Tripoli;
We fight our country's battles
On the land as on the sea;
First to fight for right and freedom
And to keep our honor clean;
We are proud to claim the title
Of United States Marine.
Our flag's unfurled to every breeze
From dawn to setting sun;
We have fought in ev'ry clime and place
Where we could take a gun;
In the snow of far-off Northern lands
And in sunny tropic scenes;
You will find us always on the job
The United States Marines
Here's health to you and to our Corps
Which we are proud to serve;
In many a strife we've fought for life
And never lost our nerve;
If the Army and the Navy
Ever look on Heaven's scenes;
They will find the streets are guarded
By United States Marines.

www.ingramcontent.com/pod-product-compliance
Lightning Source LLC
Chambersburg PA
CBHW070223030726
47505CB00006B/1799